Whiskey River Rockstar

Whiskey River Rockstar

A Whiskey River Romance

Justine Davis

TULE
PUBLISHING

Whiskey River Rockstar
Copyright © 2018 Justine Davis
Tule Publishing First Printing, March 2018

The Tule Publishing Group, LLC

ALL RIGHTS RESERVED

First Publication by Tule Publishing Group 2018

No part of this book may be used or reproduced in any manner whatsoever without written permission except in the case of brief quotations embodied in critical articles and reviews.

This is a work of fiction. Names, characters, places, and incidents are products of the author's imagination or are used fictitiously. Any resemblance to actual events, locales, organizations, or persons, living or dead, is entirely coincidental.

ISBN: 978-1-948342-66-7

Chapter One

I WONDER IF *they know I can hear them?*

The man sitting on the floor with his back to the corner wondered it only idly, since it made no difference. They weren't saying anything he didn't already know. He didn't look up, just continued to stare at the floor tiles, as if the swirled pattern of brown and tan and white held all the answers to the world, when in fact it looked like an amateurish effort from a barista trainee.

The words rained down on him like the stinging hail of a Texas storm.

Another one. Damned drugs.

Nobody forced him to take them.

But what a loss, so much talent. I love their music.

Waste is waste, and I have no patience for it.

He kept his head down. He didn't want them to realize he was there, jammed into this corner, waiting for the official word of what he already knew in his gut. They'd probably feel bad if they knew. Or maybe not. Maybe they were so inured to it they didn't feel anything anymore. He almost hoped that was the case, for their sakes. He couldn't imagine dealing with tragedy day after day and feeling full bore about it all the time.

They walked away then, still talking, but about something else. It had been the man who had been saying he loved Scorpions On Top music, and the woman writing them off. He tried to seize on that, analyze it, wondering if there was some great significance there. He didn't have the energy or the drive to even complete the thought.

He heard heavy footsteps approaching. Glanced only high enough to see feet that weren't—thankfully—clad in hospital-type shoes or clogs. Boots. Battered, scuffed, with the buckle on the left one missing. From which came the nickname that was used by all.

The bass player dropped down beside him on the floor. "No word?"

He shook his head. Still without looking up.

"I don't get it," Boots said.

He had nothing to say, and didn't. Followed a swirl of white on the floor that, apparently by chance, met with an adjacent tile to continue a stream.

"Wonder where he got it? I didn't see any of the usuals around."

The white spread into a blotch that looked vaguely like a dragonfly. Or maybe a skinny seagull, if its wings were shredded.

"And why tonight?" Boots asked, his voice thick with confusion. "It was a smoking show. Damn near perfect."

At last he lifted his gaze. Boots looked a bit shell-shocked. He supposed he did, too. Slowly, he shook his head, went back to studying the floor.

After a while Boots shifted, crossed his legs, pulled a guitar pick out of his pocket and began his familiar routine of moving it over and under his fingers, from little finger to thumb and back again. He didn't use it to play, kept it only for this purpose. There was something soothing about the movements, and Boots' dexterity with the pick.

The motion stopped. Boots took the pick between his thumb and forefinger and held it up. Stared at it. They exchanged a look, as if they'd both suddenly remembered it belonged to the man behind those doors. Boots shoved it back in his pocket.

"He might need it."

He didn't say not to bother, that the owner wouldn't be needing a pick or anything else again. Ever. If the guy needed to hope, let him.

"You know," Boots said, his voice rough, "you're the only one of us I never worried about pulling this kind of thing."

He shrugged, his shoulders rubbing against the walls of his corner. He had sampled the excesses now and then—it was hard not to in this world, especially at the heady height the band had been at lately. But he'd never done much, and that not often.

"You're always so centered," Boots added.

Centered. Interesting word. Was he? Was he centered?

Was that what kept him level, and away from most of the excesses? Or was it simpler than that? Was it something in his blood, his memory, his life that kept him on an even keel for the most part? The memories of how easy it was to lose everything? Or people who would never forgive him if he threw it all away? An image flashed through his mind, of a pair of vivid blue eyes looking at him warningly.

"You're different," Boots said. "Only drug you ever needed was the music."

He met and held the bassist's gaze at last. "That's what I don't get," he said, hearing the pain echoing in his own voice as he glanced toward the double doors that led into the emergency room. "Why isn't the music enough?"

If Boots had an answer, he didn't have a chance to give it. The doors swung open, and this time it was the shoes and scrubs he'd dreaded. The ER doctor was young, but her eyes already looked old. And they spoke it all before she said the words.

"I'm sorry."

"Zinnia Rose Mahan!"

Zee snapped out of the reverie she hadn't realized she'd slipped into at the sound of her brother's exasperated voice. She dropped her pen on the desk and looked up at him.

"What?"

"Boy, I know you're down deep when it takes that name to snap you out of it."

He was grinning at her. All the insufferable idiot did these days was grin. But why shouldn't he? He'd found Hope, hadn't he? Literally and figuratively? And she didn't begrudge him, not one tiny bit. Of all people, True deserved to be happy. He was the most honorable, stand-up guy she'd ever known, and she'd been afraid when Amanda had died he'd never try again. But Hope Larson had changed all that, and her brother was nearly delirious with newfound happiness. And Hope herself had blossomed, shedding the fear she'd carried for so long the moment she'd finally taken a stand to face what she'd run from.

"Just thinking," Zee said, making an effort not to sound defensive. She'd apparently been lost since her phone had signaled her when she'd gotten back into the office, after returning to the kitchen because she'd forgotten her coffee.

She'd heard it the moment she picked up the steaming mug for a sip. It had been a while since that particular notification had sounded. The tone was a guitar riff from one of Scorpions On Top's first hits, the combination of Texas roots, blues, and an inventive dash of rock having caught the ears of millions. She'd assigned the riff to the search she had set up to run regularly, looking for news about them. This morning it had been a review of last night's benefit concert in L.A., a glowing appraisal of what had apparently been a stellar three-hour show that left even their most strident fans sated and happy.

She told herself tracking them had nothing to do with the fact that she had once had a fierce crush on—okay, more than that, she'd been in love with—the man who had started and led the band, Jamie Templeton. It was simply to keep up with the hometown boy made good. As she was sure many in Whiskey River did, out of sheer pride in one of their own, riding high under the bright lights.

But deep down she knew she'd done it out of fear. Fear of what she might read some day.

"You're thinking even when you're not," True teased, once more dragging her back to the moment.

She gave him a wry, one-cornered smile. "You wanted something?"

"A favor."

"Sure."

"A big favor," he warned.

Uh-oh. "Ask," she said cautiously.

"I've got that meeting with the county guy for the sign-off on the pavilion this morning."

Her brows lowered. She knew that, and she knew he knew that she—She broke off the string. "Hello? I made the appointment?"

"I know. But I also have a delivery coming."

"Is that all?" She often did that, was present for a delivery when True couldn't be. It was no big deal, so she didn't get why—

Damn.

"Millie's place," she said flatly. And with certainty; it was the only thing that would make him classify such a routine thing as a "big" favor.

"Yes."

"It has to be the same time?"

"It's this morning or a week from now." Which would, Zee knew, throw their whole schedule into a scramble. "Sorry, Zee, but it was the only time they had clear."

"Fine."

Her brother looked at her warily, knowing perfectly well that had been one of *those*—a "fine" that meant anything but. "Hope offered, but they have a new group of kids coming in for the outreach today."

For a moment her mood lightened. It was like her soon to be sister-in-law to do that. Zee was coming to like Hope more and more for herself, as well as for her obvious love for her brother. "She's a treasure, bro."

"Yes. She is."

She would have done much more than go wait for a delivery, even there, for that smile and the look in his eyes. Ironic that she was dreading going to the very place True had found the woman who had so changed his life.

Millie Templeton's place. She refused to call it Jamie's, although he owned it now, after the death of his livewire aunt. She had left him everything, but what she'd given him in life mattered much more. For it was Millie who had gotten him through the horrible years after the accident, and who had noticed and fostered his talent. She'd been a sort of stand-in mother for Zee herself, when she needed female advice, and for True when he needed advice about females. For a woman who'd had no children of her own, she'd acquired three that awful night.

She gave herself an inward shake; there was nothing to be gained by dwelling on that old pain. When her brother had gone, she leaned back in her chair and shoved her tousled dark bangs off her forehead. Then she set about gathering a couple of things she could do while waiting for the delivery. Knowing Charlie, he'd probably be at the end of the two-hour window he'd given, so she didn't rush. Still, she got there barely two minutes past the start time. She stayed in her car, having no desire to get out and look at the sad house she'd spent time in as a kid. And especially avoiding looking toward the big post oak on the river side, even though she couldn't see the tree house from here.

She realized she'd been twisting her ring, the topaz birthstone ring her mother had given her, and stopped. She picked up the file folder she'd grabbed, to go through the last batch of receipts True had tossed in the box. A box that was now empty and could be replaced with a much smaller in-tray, thanks to Hope clearing out years' worth of paperwork. She found herself smiling as she set aside the now organized file she would scan when she got back to the office. Hope had straightened out more than one mess since the day True had found her hiding in this abandoned place.

She liked the feel of smiling, so she avoided looking at the run-down house that had once been the prettiest on this stretch of road. Millie had been an avid gardener, and it had shown when her roses had been blooming and the morning glories growing about a foot a day. She hated that Jamie had let it go. She really thought he had cared more than that, but obviously she'd been wrong. Wouldn't be the first—

A notification from her phone interrupted the train of thought that had already headed downhill. It always did when it came to Jamie Templeton.

For a moment she just stared at her purse, at the pocket that held the phone. This was twice today she'd heard that riff, and that seemed…something that she should get again it now, sitting here of all places.

She fished it out, unlocked the screen and tapped the notification icon. Reception wasn't the best out here, so it spun for a moment before starting to load. Then it did it in pieces, the headline and then the subhead. And then it died completely, the connection dropped. But there was enough. Too much.

She stared. She felt surprisingly numb, but then she'd expected this from the day Jamie had left Whiskey River for good, chasing the big success he and his band had managed in amazingly short order.

Scorpions On Top Loses Front Man

Jamie Templeton: The 27 Curse Strikes Again?

It had finally happened.

She dropped the phone in her lap as the pain burst through.

Chapter Two

"Zee?" She heard the tap and the call from the inner doorway, but couldn't seem to answer. She wasn't even sure how she'd managed to get home, and she was sure Charlie thought she'd gone crazy. She had no idea what she'd even said to him, and he'd hurried out of there as soon as he'd offloaded the shingles.

She stayed curled up in the big chair in the living room, the most she could manage a glance that way as the door swung open. Her brother's fiancée came through into her side of the big house True had divided into comfortable homes for both of them. They'd grown up in this house—it had come to them when their parents had been killed—and while it was very different now that it was two homes rather than one, there was still a sort of comfort in that. Just as there was comfort in this big, overstuffed chair that had been her father's.

And she needed comfort just now.

Hope paused next to Zee's cell phone that lay, screen

shattered, on the floor where it had fallen after she had thrown it with some ferocity against the granite counter in the kitchen. And being Hope, she knelt to pick it up.

"Expensive and very stupid temper tantrum," Zee said from her chair.

Hope set the now non-functional phone on the kitchen counter. "Sometimes a girl's gotta do what a girl's gotta do."

Zee drew in a deep breath, the first she'd really been able to. And nearly managed a smile. No wonder True was so happy. If Hope could make her feel like almost smiling when inside she felt nauseous to the point of vomiting…

She watched as the petite woman with the long, dark reddish hair and cinnamon eyes crossed the room toward her, and then again knelt beside her chair. There was vivid concern in those eyes, and Zee knew it was genuine. Hope had left her days of pretending all was well far behind her.

"I thought you had a new group at the outreach."

"We did. Deck got free and came over, so they're busy either peppering him with questions about the next Sam Smith adventure, or working very hard to seem cool and totally unimpressed that they're chatting with a world-famous author."

Zee did smile at that. And for that alone she said a soft "Thank you."

"You've missed some calls."

"I don't want to talk to anyone."

"I get that. But True's been trying to call you."

Zee's glance flicked to her now non-functional cell phone. "He sent you?"

"He said—"

Hope broke off as her own cell rang. She fished it out of her back pocket, and Zee just had time to see the image attached to the caller. True.

"I'm with her," Hope said without preamble. So, True had sent her. Which answered her other question. He had heard.

Hope went suddenly still. "You're sure?" And then she smiled, widely, although it faded as if she'd suddenly thought of something that made it inappropriate.

Hope held out the phone. Zee shook her head. She didn't want to hear even her beloved brother's efforts at consolation, condolences, or whatever he thought she needed just now.

"Trust me," Hope said.

Reluctantly she took it. Raised it to her ear. "I don't want to hear it, Truett," she said, using his full name for emphasis.

True didn't waste time with niceties. "It wasn't him, Zee."

She froze, for a moment forgot to even breathe. "What?"

"It wasn't Jamie."

"But they said—"

"I know. They got it wrong. They do that a lot, if you haven't noticed."

"Then the ones saying it isn't him could be wrong—"

"I talked to him, Zee."

The knot inside her shattered, and she felt as if the shards had sliced through every muscle in her body. A chill swept her, followed by a glorious warmth.

"Oh, God," she whispered.

"It was Derek. The new guitarist."

She couldn't speak. She didn't like that she was relieved at a man's death, but she had never met the guy.

"Jamie was there, in the ER with him, so that's probably how it got confused."

She made a sound that didn't resemble a word.

"He didn't call you?" True asked. "I told him to, or I'd fly out there and kick his ass. He said he would."

"I...my phone's broken."

There was a slight pause. As if he'd guessed how it had gotten broken. But being True, he said only, "Call him. Use Hope's phone if yours is broken."

"I..." She pulled herself together. Told herself that because disaster had been avoided once didn't mean it still wouldn't happen.

"Zee, call him. He's really rattled. I think he might need a Zinnia Rose chewing out."

"He should be rattled!" And it suddenly hit her why Hope's smile had faded; for somebody's family, the disaster had struck. She'd felt the same way Zee had. A bit guilty at being happy it was somebody else.

"I know. I know. But it's Jamie, Zee. He's still Jamie. However it ended between you, he—"

"I told you, we were friends, that's all, and—"

"Right. Did you think just because Amanda and I were trying to get pregnant and quit using them that I wouldn't eventually notice the condoms you stole?"

Zee felt herself flush, even as she felt a flash of gratitude toward Hope; it was only because of her that True was able to even talk about Amanda and those efforts so evenly.

"Besides, you were way too mad at him for just a friend leaving town."

"You never said anything."

"What was I going to do, lecture you? Go all big brother on him? I trusted him to be careful with you. He swore he would never lie to you, and you've said he didn't."

"It's true. He didn't."

"Hell, Zee, our parents were dead. I sucked at being a father figure. I knew you were probably too young, but I was all for either of us finding some happy wherever we could. And Jamie made you happy."

He had made her happy. And he had been careful. Deliciously careful.

He'd also given her every chance to stop him, even pushed her to change her mind before they'd made such incredible discoveries together. And he'd never lied to her, never said he would stay. He'd been honest even when it hurt. Perhaps most of all when it hurt.

"I'll call him," she finally said.

"Good. Hope will stay with you, if you want."

"I'm sure she'll be thrilled to hear that."

"She offered," he said again. "And I'll be home in a couple of hours."

"I'll be fine."

"Still. See you later."

"Yes. And, bro?"

"What?"

"You never, ever sucked at being a father figure."

She ended the call before he could make his usual protest. Zee lifted her gaze to her soon to be sister-in-law. Hope was smiling, this time fully and clearly heartfelt.

"But he really does suck at taking compliments," Zee said.

Hope laughed. "He does." She reached out, put a hand over Zee's. "How about some ice cream for strength before you make that call?"

To her surprise, Zee found herself laughing. "No wonder you and I get along."

HE COULDN'T DENY the ache any longer. Or the need. In the rest of his life he didn't have the slightest idea what he wanted to do now, but in this one thing he was certain.

Jamie Templeton wanted to go home.

He stared at the sparkling water in the pool behind the canyon house he and Boots had been renting for the past year. It gave the illusion of being secluded, but an illusion was all it was; the moment you stepped out front you could see the tumble of houses jammed along the road, all tinder for the next wildfire that hit these hills above Los Angeles. Back home, a wildfire could burn a few acres and take out a house or two; here it could burn the same area and take out dozens.

Back home. He even thought the words with longing.

The guys—and Leigh, their keyboardist—wouldn't be surprised. He'd been talking about it for a while. Enough that they'd begun to tease him about being homesick for the wide-open spaces. He didn't tell them his homesickness was much more specific than that. It was for the town he'd grown up in, the little house he'd once called home, the sight of the river from a tree house.

And the woman who'd made his music possible. But it was too late for her now.

I'm sorry, Aunt Millie. I should have stayed home.

That she had been the first one to urge him to chase his dream, the one who had taken such pride in his success, who in fact had given the band its name with her old joke about opening a can of worms and finding scorpions on top, didn't ease the stab of guilt. He should have stayed with her all the time when she'd gotten sick. He owed her so much. He'd missed his parents horribly, but she'd made life bearable, and eventually, helped him find the reason to go on. She'd bought him that first guitar, a sweet-sounding acoustic that had lived with him in that tree house that first summer after the accident. She'd found him a teacher, and paid for the lessons. And only later did she admit to him that she left a window open on the river side of the house, even in hot Texas summers, so she could hear him practice.

That she had insisted he go, told him he'd made commitments and had to honor them, didn't ease it, either. Even though he knew she'd meant it; keeping your word was a big thing for her. Just like it was for Zee…

Zee.

If he went home he would see her. Often. There was no way to avoid it. And she would likely be as mad at him as she'd been the last time he'd seen her. When they'd gathered to help Hope.

That hometown feeling was what he'd missed. In that case, since he hadn't known Hope yet, it had been to pay back a little to True, who had done so much for him and almost everybody in town. But it was the nature of Whiskey River, too. When one of their own really needed help, they pulled together like no place he'd ever seen anywhere else. He was sure there must be other towns like that, but Whiskey River was his.

If you meant that, you'd come home more often.

Zee's words, spoken at Millie's funeral, dug at him more often than he cared to admit. But then, she'd always been able to get to him like no one else. In every way. He hadn't realized that at seventeen, but ever since he'd left he'd discovered that no one else, no other woman, made him feel the way she had. He'd tried to write it off as nostalgia, a faulty memory of how good it had been. But deep down some part of him knew the bar had forever been set too high.

And he'd left her behind.

He hadn't lied to her. At least he didn't have that worst kind of guilt riding him. He'd made it clear, back when they'd been teenagers with hormones running high and had taken that final step together, that he was still leaving. In fact, he'd given a decent amount of energy to try and convince her she didn't want to take that last step with him, not when he'd be gone soon. At the time he'd felt almost noble about it. A lot of guys would have just grabbed what she was offering and left town—and her—feeling smug.

He'd never felt smug around Zee. Because he knew how damned smart she was. And clear-headed. Usually. Except for him. Because if she had been clear-headed around him, those sweet, hot Texas nights might never have happened.

Well, that'll be something to tell the kids someday, that my first time was in a tree house.

Her words that night, as the soft breeze dried the sweat on naked skin, had sent a ripple of unease through him. And being Zee, she had sensed it.

Relax, jumpy boy. I didn't necessarily mean our *kids.*

Yeah, smart was the word. So maybe she had known

what she was doing. She sure as hell had known what she wanted.

Him.

The thought made him shiver despite the sunshine that sparkled off the pool. Never had he been so sure a woman wanted him, the real him, not some image they'd built up in their mind. Not some stage-lit hero they thought they knew because they related or responded to his music. Or worse, because to them just being on that stage made him sexy, desirable, and who he really was didn't matter.

And right now he'd give just about anything to be sitting in that damned tree house.

"Damn, it's bright out here."

Boots sat down beside him, rubbing at his eyes. They'd thrown a bit of a wake for Derek last night, and the aftereffects lingered. Most of yesterday was a blur anyway.

"Yeah."

"You talk to Rob?"

"Yeah."

"Tour's over?"

"Yeah."

They had reached the level where they were a cottage industry of their own—sound and light guys, managers of various aspects, publicists, merchandise sellers and assorted others. And his decision would affect them all, so he'd thought long and hard before he'd done it, but in the end there had been no other decision he could make. And he'd told Rob Finlay, their business manager, this morning. Or maybe it had been afternoon. He wasn't clear on that.

"You're leaving, aren't you."

This time it wasn't a question. And for the first time he said it out loud. "Yes. I'm going home."

After a moment Boots nodded. "Be good for all of us to take a break."

Jamie only nodded in turn. Would it be only a break? Or a permanent end? He didn't know.

"Maybe later, Ronnie might want to come back, at least for a while," Boots said, referring to the player Derek had replaced. The tall, lanky guitarist had become a producer of some note, in demand, and enjoyed it enough that he'd left the road behind.

"After they fly Derek home, the plane'll take you guys…wherever. If you want."

"How about Hawaii?" Boots was clearly trying for a lighter tone, but it rang a bit hollow.

"If you want," Jamie repeated.

"Going back to your girl back home?"

Jamie's breath jammed up in his throat. He turned his head to stare at the man who was his closest friend in this crazy business.

Boots shrugged. "Figured there had to be somebody. I mean, relatively speaking, you're the damned straightest arrow I've ever run into in this business. Especially for a front man."

"You say that like it's a bad thing," Jamie said, trying to steer Boots off the subject of girls back home.

"Just rare. She must really be something."

He shrugged in turn. *So much for subject changes.*

After a moment Boots said, "Your phone's flashing like a strobe in there."

"Figured."

"Not going to answer anybody?"

"I talked to everybody…almost everybody I wanted to. And Derek's family. That's all I care about at the moment. And the media can go hang."

"I'll hold the rope," Boots said with a grimace. "You gonna go to the funeral Sunday?"

Jamie closed his eyes. It was the last thing he wanted. But he would. "Yes."

"Sucks, man."

"Yeah."

And all the sunshine in California couldn't change that.

Chapter Three

*T*RUE SAYS YOU'RE *worried. Don't be. You've still got me to be mad at. Someday maybe you'll tell me the real reason why.*

Zee didn't know why she kept listening to that stupid message. The first time it had been merely to confirm—because she knew her brother would ask—that he'd done as True had told him and called. And it was his voice, with that low, slightly rough quality that made her feel as if he'd brushed guitar-toughened fingers over her skin. But his tone was hardly pleasant. It was short, the words clipped. It lacked any of Jamie's natural charm, and certainly wasn't something she wanted to hear repeatedly, in either tone or content.

And yet she kept playing it. And had been since she'd gotten the replacement phone she'd had to wait for, and been able to check voice mails.

Someday maybe you'll tell me the real reason why.

The real reason? Seriously?

No, that wasn't fair. He'd been ever honest. He'd never, ever told her he would stay. The opposite in fact. He'd made it very clear he'd be gone as soon as he could manage it. And when she'd decided with all the foolishness of her young heart—and body—that her first lover simply had to be him, she'd told herself she was all right with it.

You don't want to do this, Zee. Not with me, not when I'm hitting the road as soon as the band is ready.

She'd brushed off his noble impulse. *I'll deal with that then.*

It wasn't his fault that afterward, she couldn't believe he still meant to go. Because what they'd found together was so amazing she couldn't believe anyone would leave it voluntarily.

Of course, there was always the possibility it hadn't been quite so amazing for him. That idea had hovered since the day he'd done exactly as he'd said and left Whiskey River in the rearview mirror. And it had only added to her turmoil.

You were way too mad at him...

Her brother's words jabbed at her anew. She let out a short, sharp breath. Did every male in her life think they had her figured out? Although Jamie wasn't really in her life. Not anymore. Because he hadn't been able to wait to get out of Whiskey River, for all his declarations that he loved his hometown.

Belatedly she realized the sound she'd made sounded suspiciously like a huff. And she refused to be That Woman, the kind who whined when a man did exactly what he said he was going to do.

Spurred by a jolt of self-disgust, she belatedly kept her promise to True and made that call. And couldn't deny the burst of relief she felt when it went straight to voice mail, as if the phone had been turned off. She was greeted by the pre-installed mechanical voice announcing only the number she had reached and to leave a message. She supposed he'd done that to preclude anyone who hit the number by accident from realizing who they'd actually gotten.

"It's Zee. I got your message. Thank you for calling. I'll tell my brother you kept your word." She hesitated, not sure what else to say. "Sorry about your friend."

She disconnected, knowing it was abrupt, but if she'd kept going she was afraid she'd say something she'd regret.

She walked over to the window, looked out at the quiet street. She would have understood it better if he'd hated it here. If the memories made it too painful to stay. That she could live with. She'd wondered herself if she might be happier someplace else, with fewer memories. But Whiskey River was her home and had her heart. She could never leave her brother, the only family she had left, and when it came right down to it she couldn't imagine living anywhere else anyway.

Apparently Jamie couldn't imagine living here. And she supposed that was the crux of it; she was having trouble accepting that the boy she'd loved so passionately didn't exist anymore. That on top of it all he'd become a hypocrite, writing and singing songs about home and how much he missed it, but avoiding it as if he loathed every inch of it.

That it still mattered to her was infuriating, but the nausea and chill that had overtaken her when she'd read that mistaken headline—fine lot of good their retraction and apology an hour later had done—was undeniable. Apparently all her efforts to dissociate herself from the Hometown Boy Made Good had been for nothing.

Her mouth tightened and she made herself focus on what she should have been doing instead of listening to that silly message. She finished setting up the new phone with her preferred notification tones—leaving the Scorpions riffs, after some hesitation—and re-downloading some apps that hadn't made the transfer properly. The only thing she didn't duplicate was the search and alert feature assigned to the band. That, at least, she would break herself of. She—

The knock on the inside door was True's decisive rap. Hope's was lighter, quicker, her brother's solid and stronger. Just as they themselves were.

"Open," she called out.

The moment he stepped in she wished she'd kept her mouth shut. One look at his face told her she wasn't going to like whatever he said. And True-like, he cut to the chase.

"I'm heading to Devil's Rock. Jamie's coming in."

"Lucky you." There. Her voice had been nicely neutral. "Coming home to lick his wounds? Lucky Whiskey River." The dispassionate tone wobbled slightly. True tactfully ignored it.

"He was coming anyway, for the wedding. Now it's just a little early. Do you want to come along?"

She blinked. Lost the neutrality completely. "Why on earth would I?"

"Because," her brother said, "nobody else knows he's coming yet, and I thought you might want to see him the first time in…controlled circumstances."

"Controlled?"

"As in not half of Whiskey River looking on. Shouldn't be many at the airfield on a Tuesday afternoon."

"I did fine on the Hope flight."

That's what they'd taken to calling the marshaling of forces to help Hope take her life back. And Jamie had been front and center in their little army—she'd had to admit that—providing the sleek little jet that had flown them all to L.A. where Hope had, with a half-dozen of them at her back plus two more added on the other end, faced down and ended the trouble that had sent her on the run.

"Fine if you don't count staring darts at him the whole way."

"I didn't."

"Okay, most of the way."

She knew she was arguing with him to stall for time to think. Because he had a point. As her brother usually did. It just might be better to have her first encounter with Jamie—and it would happen because Whiskey River wasn't that big—someplace more private than, say, in front of Booze's statue in the town square. With her luck Martha, the town gossip, would be passing at just that moment. And no matter how much she told herself she was over him, it wouldn't be the kind of friendly, happy greeting old friends reunited would be expected to have. She wasn't *that* strong.

"Get it over with, sis," True said.

"Did you tell him? That I might be coming?"

Her brother's mouth quirked. "You mean did I warn him? No. I only said we'd be there to meet him. I didn't say which 'we.' I love him like a brother, but you are my sister."

"And you are ever loyal," she said softly, diverted for a moment by this man she was lucky enough to have for a sibling. "Hope is a lucky woman."

"I'm the lucky one."

"You're both about to make me gag." She smiled to take any edge out of it.

"And Jamie's the only one who has ever put my rock-solid sister on tenterhooks."

"What is a tenterhook, anyway?"

"And he's the only one who can make you dodge like that."

She let out an exasperated breath. "All right, all right. I'll go. Get it over with, as you said."

"Good."

"But don't blame me if he gets ticked at you for bringing me."

True grimaced. "I'll be hiding out in the hangar."

"And what makes you think we won't both come after you?"

True's voice was suddenly very serious. "I'd welcome it. Just to see you two united again."

They took her car for the back seat, but she told True to drive. Which gave Zee time to think about his words all the way out to Devil's Rock, the airfield named for the distinctive rock formation at one end of the runway. Could it be possible? Could they reach a sort of peace?

She signed inwardly. She knew who would have to let go for that to happen. Because she was certain, in his mind, Jamie had nothing to let go of. So he didn't mean those songs—so what? They were still beautiful. He'd hit it big. It was too much to expect him to hang out in little Whiskey River. And she was glad for him, truly, he'd had a dream and he'd made it happen.

They heard the plane before they spotted it. They watched the sleek little jet circle for an approach. This was hardly a busy airfield, but things were happening here and it might not stay that way for long. Zee wondered if Keely Rockford was at the controls. She'd met the woman briefly on the Hope flight, and had been impressed with her easy demeanor and quiet skill as a pilot. She'd learned then that Jamie always requested her when they used the service, which was often enough that this aircraft was used almost exclusively by the band.

As the plane touched down—smooth and steady, she noted—she wondered where the rest of them were, those talented musicians who had lost one of their own.

"Is this just him?" she asked, thinking she should have thought of it before.

"Yes," True said, watching as the jet taxied their way. "He sent everybody else wherever they wanted to go first."

"Oh."

True glanced at her. "He's still a good guy, Zee."

"Just not the guy who left here seven years ago."

"Of course not. He was barely twenty. And none of us are the person we were then."

She could not argue that. But she had the feeling Jamie had changed more than any of them. How could he not, given the world he had dived into so whole-heartedly?

They walked over when the little jet came to a halt. Zee could see it was indeed Keely in the cockpit. A couple of minutes later, she took in a deep breath when the hatch door opened. Steadied herself. She would stay cool, greet him like anyone else would, and then the worst would be over. Her tangled emotions were her fault, not his.

To her surprise, it was Keely who emerged first. Tall, trim, and California tan, she looked as she had before: cool, professional, and competent. Her dark hair was pulled back in a simple tail at the back of her neck today. She spotted them, and came quickly down the steps.

"I'm glad you're here," she said quietly. "He needs home right now."

True nodded. "I got the feel."

"I've been flying them nearly a year now, and I've never

seen him like this," Keely said. "The others are in rough shape, the shock and all, but Jamie…he's been in a mood for a while, but now he's…"

Zee frowned as the woman ended with a slow shake of her head. Jamie was nothing if not resilient. And he hadn't known the new guy all that long. But she and True knew better than most, having gone through it twice, that losing people never got easier.

And then there was a movement in the hatchway. She looked up, thinking herself braced for her first glimpse of him.

But there was no way she could have braced for what she saw.

…not the guy who left here seven years ago.

Her words, it seemed, had been a vast understatement. This wasn't even the guy who had flown in here two months ago. His eyes were hollow, with dark circles beneath them. He had always tended toward the lean, rangy side, but now he was even leaner, to the point of gauntness. He even moved differently, his easy, supple grace seemingly vanished as he made his way almost hesitantly down the steps, slightly bent as if the weight of the single guitar case slung over his shoulder was much greater than she knew it likely was. An image of him from two months ago, when he'd agilely deplaned sliding with his hands on the rails and never touching the steps shot through her mind. Any trace of that nimble man was gone.

But most of all, what was missing was that crackling, vivid charisma that charmed without effort, because it was inborn in him. There was no trace of it now, no easy, captivating smile, no flash of fun and invitation to join in shone in those green eyes that looked strangely flat. The upbeat, confident guy who was on top of the world was nowhere to be seen.

She didn't doubt now that Keely had been right—there was more going on. As if Derek's senseless death had been the final catalyst.

This Jamie Templeton was nothing but a hollow shell.

Chapter Four

JAMIE NEARLY STUMBLED when he saw her. When True had said they'd be here, he'd assumed he meant Hope would be with him. Not his sister.

Not Zee.

Damn, he wasn't ready for this. He hadn't slept more than a couple of hours at a time in the past five days, and he was in no shape to deal with her anger at him. Especially when deep down there was that part of him that resented that she was mad at him. He'd never lied to her, never promised her anything beyond the moment. And yet she acted as if he'd jilted her at the altar, or died on her or something. Died. Damn.

Sorry, Aunt Millie.

It was a reflex thought; his beloved aunt never spoke of her ill-fated love that had ended in a battle-torn place overseas. She had never married, but insisted she was happy. Because, she'd said, she'd gotten something wonderful out of life after all.

Him.

You wouldn't think so now, Aunt Millie.

And now they were both dead. And he was standing here staring at Zee, who had once been the most wonderful thing in his life.

He recovered and traversed the rest of the steps. True took one look at him and reached out to take the guitar. He thought about resisting, but he trusted the man and he didn't have the energy or strength anyway. And it took all he had of both to make himself look at Zee.

She was staring, looking as if she was in shock. He knew he looked like hell, and up until he saw that look in her vivid blue eyes, he hadn't much cared.

"Please," he said, not even sure what he was pleading for.

After a moment Zee nodded. As if she'd understood what he hadn't been able to find words for. But then, she always had been good at that.

Keely had grabbed his duffel and backpack, all he'd brought beside the guitar, and brought them over. True took the duffel; Zee grabbed the pack before he could reach for it.

"We'll look out for him," True said to the pilot, and he vaguely wondered what Keely had said to them that had brought that on. She reached out and put a hand on his arm. He reflexively looked at her, saw her eyes were full of concern.

"Take care of yourself," she said. "Or better yet, let them."

She was not usually so demonstrative. Another measure

of how bad he must look, he guessed. "Thank you," he said, at a loss for any other words.

"Just in case," she said softly, "it's been a pleasure."

He knew what she meant. That she realized what decision he was on the precipice of. With an effort he put some more words together. "I hope we weren't too much trouble."

She smiled at him. "Believe me, I've flown trouble. You guys ain't it."

He managed a fleeting smile back at her. "Thanks for getting the guys…where they wanted to go."

She nodded. "This is a good place, Jamie. Let it heal you."

He was tapped out and could only nod.

"If you ever need anything," True said, and Jamie realized he was talking to Keely.

"Thank you," she said with a nod. "I know you mean that. I saw that last time." She glanced around at the airfield, as if looking beyond it. "This is a good place," she said again.

"It is," Zee said. "We'll take care of him."

Jamie registered that she'd said it without malice, or any of the antagonism he usually got from her. And there was something in her eyes that he hadn't seen in a very long time, something beside the concern she would show any injured creature. Which is what he felt like just now. He managed to get to the car. Barely. Zee's car? He thought it must be. True drove a work truck.

He put a hand on the roof of the car—a practical green

sedan, nothing flashy except the color, which was a bit brighter than the oak leaves this spring—to steady himself. True popped the trunk and put the bags in. He thought foggily he should tell him not the guitar, but then saw he didn't have to; True had closed the trunk without putting the case in, knowing somehow he'd want it with him.

"Are you on something? Using?" He stared at True, blinked rather slowly at the abrupt and unexpected question. "Do we need to get a doctor?"

Oh. "I...no. Don't. Not for a long time."

"When was the last time you slept?" Zee asked. Slowly he shifted his gaze to her face. Her voice had matched that look in her eyes, and a shiver went through him. He hadn't realized how much he'd missed the Zee who wasn't mad at him.

"Last night," he got out.

"For how long?"

"Couple hours." She just looked at him. "If you add it up," he said.

"A couple of hours in the last week, I'm guessing," she said briskly. "Get in the back. Lie down."

"I—"

"Just do it, Jamie."

His name. She'd said his name. Softly. Without that edge in her voice. He felt like she'd stroked him. He did as she asked. He'd do anything she asked, when she talked to him like that.

He was asleep before the car started.

"Where are we taking him?"

True gave her a sideways look, then glanced at the backseat.

"He's out for the count," she said.

"And looks like hell."

"Yes. He does."

"It's been a rough week for him."

"Yes. But…"

"What?" True asked.

"It's more than that. Derek dying, I mean. Not that that's not bad enough, but…I can see that it's more than that. I sensed something even when he was here in March, for Hope. Under all the charm, something was wrong."

"I'll never argue with you when it comes to understanding him. You always did."

"For all the good it—" She stopped the words. That quiet, almost desperate plea flashed through her mind. And only now did she realize what a reflex being mad at Jamie Templeton had become.

"You never were one to kick a guy when he's down."

She met her brother's gaze. "I shouldn't be kicking him at all. He never promised me anything."

"And it's been seven years."

"Yes."

"Still raw, though?"

"Only when I think about it."

"I'd say take his stuff out of your song rotation, but I get the feeling it would only remind you why it wasn't there and you'd be back to square one."

Her mouth quirked. "For a guy, you're pretty smart, bro."

"Wow, thanks a lot," True said, but he was fighting a smile.

"It'd help if he wasn't so damned good."

"So he deserved that award, huh?"

Zee flushed despite herself. The day last summer when a big online music site had given Jamie their "The Rocker We'd Most Like to F♥♥♥"—they'd actually used the damned little hearts—award had been a rough one for her. It was the day she'd finally let go of any dream or hope she'd had that he would someday come home. He was well and truly of that world now, with little trace of the boy from Whiskey River left.

"I meant his music," she ground out.

"So did I," True said blandly. "I meant the *Beat Magazine* award, of course."

"Sure you did." Sometimes he was such a...a brother.

It was a rough few minutes of silence, during which she fought off the memories of those sweet nights when anything had seemed possible, even Jamie changing his mind. She should have known, in fact she had known, for even with only the accompaniment of that simple guitar, with the breeze rustling the leaves around the tree house, he had been something very, very special. And she had told him so.

You can't have it both ways, girl. You can't tell him he could go all the way and then try to hold him back.

"I'm sorry you got hurt," her brother said.

"I did it to myself," she muttered.

"Then why take it out on him?"

"Because he wasn't here."

It was a moment before True said, very carefully, "I suppose that makes sense in your mind."

"As much as anything does right now."

"Zee—"

"Don't worry. I'll go easy on him. Like you said, I don't kick a guy when he's down. And he is most assuredly that."

"Which brings us back to your original question. Where are we taking him? Aunt Millie's place obviously isn't habitable."

She shrugged. "You and Hope have an empty guest room."

"So do you."

She went still. "Oh, no, Truett Mahan. Don't you ask for that. I'll help look out for him, but I can't live with him in my house."

To his credit, he didn't push. "If our place is too close, he could probably stay with Kelsey and Deck until he figures out what he wants to do."

"But we promised we'd take care of him."

They were coming into Whiskey River now, and he slowed. He glanced at her with an odd expression. "Is this how it's been for you? This constant internal war about him?"

She let out a long breath. It sounded so…silly when he said it out loud.

"At first, when you started seeing Nick," he said, "I thought you might be past it."

"So did I." Nick had been a decent guy, and he'd genuinely cared, but their relationship had had none of the spark she knew she would need to truly put Jamie Templeton behind her.

"Zee, it's been—"

"I know." She shot him a sideways look. "Have you forgotten Amanda?"

Once he would have winced as if she'd struck him. Now, thanks to Hope, he just looked thoughtful. "No. And I never will. But that's different."

"Very. But in a way, the Jamie I knew, my Jamie, might as well have died."

"And you blame him for changing?"

"Not any longer," she said with determination. "I'm chalking it up to life's lessons and moving on."

She meant it. And when he was lying in her backseat, practically comatose, looking like a shell of himself, it was easy to believe she could do it.

Chapter Five

ZEE WAS PONDERING breakfast when a tap on the inner door made her pull her head out of the fridge and close the door. She hoped it was her brother. But even if it wasn't, she was going to stay on this even keel. No matter what.

"Come on in," she called out, glad she'd gotten dressed after her shower instead of lolling around in her bathrobe.

The door was pulled open.

Jamie.

Barefoot, hair tousled from sleep—True had practically dumped him on the guest bed when they'd gotten here, and from what he'd said this morning he hadn't stirred once—jaw stubbled, and wearing only jeans and a white T-shirt, she was sure the readers of that damned magazine would faint away at the sight of him. With his hair streaked even blonder from the California sun, the visible strip of taut, flat belly above the low-slung jeans, and those green eyes that looked not quite so bad this morning, it was easy to see why he was the guy who'd won that award.

Not that she hadn't already known. Intimately.

But somehow she took no satisfaction in being the one who'd known exactly how sexy he was first.

She shook off the images that thought sent through her mind. Schooled her voice to pleasantness.

"Feeling better?"

He jammed a hand through his hair, shoving the tangle back off his face. Funny, his hair was actually longer than hers now, the sandy blond strands brushing his collar while her dark wisps bared her neck.

"Yeah. Thanks."

"Sleep is a wondrous thing."

"I'd almost forgotten."

Like you've forgotten—Stop it!

"You needed it. You were looking a bit too zombielike. Breakfast?"

"If it's not brains."

"In that case I'll put them back in the fridge," she said without missing a beat. And he smiled. Not quite a grin, but nearly as devastating.

"You're as quick as ever," he said.

She smiled back, proud that she was able to. But his expression faded, as if it had been a fragile, fleeting thing he couldn't maintain. And once more that feeling came flooding back, that there was more wrong than she—than maybe anyone knew.

She poured him coffee, noted he still drank it black. She fixed eggs without asking how he liked them, because she knew. He smiled again when she set them before him on the bar where he'd sat down to watch her. But again it was fleeting, almost as if it were autonomic, something his muscles did without thought, and once thought intervened it faded.

"Thanks."

"I assumed they didn't fix them some exotic way in L.A. that you like better than scrambled with cheese." His gaze flicked to her face. She made sure she was smiling; it truly had been teasing, not a jab.

"No," he said, but the single syllable sounded as if he weren't convinced. She supposed she couldn't blame him. She'd been sniping at him for a long time. He took a couple of bites. "They're as good as I remember."

"Been eating about as well as you've been sleeping?" she asked after he'd quickly worked his way through the plate of eggs and two slices of bacon she'd added.

"No appetite," he admitted.

"For how long?"

His glance was sharper this time, as if she'd surprised him. After a moment he said, sounding reluctant, "A while."

So she'd been right. There was more going on here.

"Sorry about your friend, but I'm really glad the initial media reports were wrong."

He blinked. "What?"

"About it being you."

"Oh."

She watched him, her brow still furrowed, because something had come into his expression then that she didn't like much. As if he'd suddenly understood something, and the knowledge stung. "What's wrong? Besides the obvious, I mean."

He put down his fork. "You don't have to cook for me."

"I offered. And someone clearly needs to. You're too thin."

He shrugged. Got up, carried his plate, fork and mug into the kitchen and put them into the dishwasher. He hadn't gotten completely used to people picking up after him, apparently.

Then he turned to look at her. "I only came over to…say thank you."

"Thank you for what?" She didn't like the suddenly formal edge that had come into his voice.

"For…letting me come home."

"Not like I'm in charge."

All the old feelings had bubbled up in her at his use of the word *home*. All the "If you really meant its" that had peopled her mind since the moment she'd realized he had no intention of ever coming back. That she could even think that now, when he was so clearly hurting, told her rather painfully she'd let those feelings get way out of control. She was afraid they would break loose now, when she didn't want them to, and so she rather abruptly changed the subject.

"I assume my brother's off to Declan's place?"

After a moment he nodded. "Final touches, he said. And Hope is at the rescue." He paused, an odd expression coming over his face. "They seem…genuinely, truly happy together."

"Bone-deep," she said, meaning it. "She's the best thing that could have happened to him."

"I'm glad you feel that way. I know you and Amanda were close."

"I love my brother. Hope is good for him."

"So you don't feel like she's come between you?"

She frowned.

"I only meant that…it always seemed you were determined to be an unbreakable unit. Like you were determined to take care of him the way he came home and took care of you."

"I was. But she's made him happier than I ever thought I'd see him again. I would never begrudge him that."

"She's a gutsy woman. She was amazing at that trial."

"Yes. I admire her for that."

And how much of that admiration was for doing something Zee herself couldn't seem to do—put the past behind her—she didn't really want to admit. So her tone was rather brisk as she cleared the last of the cooking debris.

"What's your plan?"

"I…hadn't thought much beyond just getting here."

She stared at him. Jamie always had a plan. From his tree house to his career path, he always had a plan.

There was definitely more wrong here. But whatever it

was, he was obviously still reeling too much to deal with it right now.

"Maybe you should go back to bed for a while."

Something flickered in his eyes, something not quite hot behind the green, but it was only a flicker and quickly faded. She knew what it once would have meant, how he once would have interpreted that as an invitation to her bed, and been right. That old longing stirred, tried to rise, and she quashed it firmly. He'd come home, yes, but for all the wrong reasons, and she'd do well to remember that.

Chapter Six

"THANKS FOR THE bed last night."

True only shrugged as he made the turn to head out to Aunt Millie's. Jamie smiled inwardly at the man's standard response to a thank-you or a compliment. True just went about his business, fixing things, going out of his way for people, solving problems, helping, leaving people feeling a gratitude that couldn't be expressed simply by paying the bill. He remembered how he himself had felt when True called for help for Hope; he couldn't jump on it fast enough.

Zee had said once that her brother tried to fix everything for everyone because he hadn't been able to fix the one thing he'd truly wanted to: Amanda.

Jamie remembered her well, the sweet, generous girl everybody had loved. Including him, because on that terrible night it had been Amanda who had stepped in and taken charge until True got there. She'd seen to him as gently and lovingly as she had Zee. Much of that time was a fog in his mind, but he remembered her more than perhaps anything except the moment Aunt Millie had arrived and taken him into her arms, assuring him they were both badly wounded but they would survive.

Guilt stabbed at him. His aunt hadn't just taken in her orphaned nephew, she'd also welcomed him, poured out her own unique kind of love and support. She was ever honest with him about what was ahead, that the true path of grief was not a straight, linear one but a snarl of loops and going back the way you came. She'd been right, about all of it, and her caring but honest approach had helped him more than any of the platitudes he got from others who wanted to shield him from the reality of his parents' deaths.

It was Aunt Millie who had comforted him after his nightmares at all hours, who had never tried to hide her own tears and thus made him feel safe enough to shed his own, who refused to lie to him and say it would ever be over, and finally, on his sixteenth birthday, she had bought him that guitar. It was nothing fancy, but it had a beautiful tone and it had taught him the basics. He still had it. Always would, even though his collection had grown to about six.

It was the guitar he'd brought with him. The only one he wanted.

"How'd you and Zee do this morning?"

Snapped out of his thoughts Jamie gave True a quick glance, but he was studiously watching the road. The man was protective of his sister, even more than a typical older brother would be, because he'd raised her since she was fourteen. Hell, he'd been Jamie's own adult male role model since then, too, his own borrowed big brother.

For all the good it did. You'd be a lot better off if you'd followed his example more.

"Okay," he finally said. It was a lukewarm word for what he'd truly felt. And it didn't help that Zee was still the most... No adjectives were enough, she was simply the most woman he'd ever known. "She seemed...worried."

"About you? Yes. I think she's been worried since you left town."

"Worried? Or mad?" he asked wryly.

"They're not mutually exclusive."

Jamie sighed. "Look, about that...I...we...I never meant..." He stopped with a disgusted snort and shook his head.

"If you're dancing around telling me you two started having sex in your senior year of high school, don't bother. I know. I always knew."

"You did?" Jamie stared at the man. "You were always so protective of her. Why the hell didn't you come after me?"

True shrugged. "Being with you was the only time Zee ever smiled. I wasn't going to take that away from her. Or you, for that matter."

Well, there's that at least. So why do I still feel so defensive about it? "I was always going to leave, and she knew it."

True flicked him a glance, then went back to the road. "We all knew it. You had big plans, dreams. And the talent to carry them out." Another glance, this time with a smile.

"Zee always said Whiskey River could never contain you."

"Then why is she so mad that I left?"

"That's between you two, and I'm not playing referee."

"Great," Jamie muttered. He'd been hoping True would at least give him a clue.

"But," True added after a moment, "you might want to rethink the idea that that's all she's mad about."

Jamie didn't like the sound of that. What else could Zee be ticked at him about? They drove on in silence for a few minutes, Jamie soaking in the view as they went, the familiar things, the big pecan tree here, carefully preserved old buildings there. It took him a moment to realize what he was feeling, it had been so long. It wasn't peace, not yet—it was too soon for that—but it was a sort of calm he hadn't had for…well, he couldn't remember when. Enough of this, of being home, and maybe he could deal with Derek. And Aunt Millie's place.

Maybe even Zee.

Maybe.

His first sight of the house, from a distance, sparked an odd feeling in him. A jab of recognition, a feel of coming home, of a destination finally reached. But the closer they got, the more another feeling grew, an unease he couldn't quite name.

"Damn," he muttered as they came to a halt in the driveway.

"Told you it was rough," True said. "I got the broken

windows out and boarded up, fixed a leak—"

"No, man, it's okay. I told you to just do what was essential for now."

"I know. But I'm still sorry I didn't check on it. Time gets away."

"And you were busy. You're always busy."

"Keeps me out of trouble."

The thought of steady, solid True Mahan in any kind of trouble almost made Jamie laugh. He got out of the truck, and for a moment just looked at the house where he'd lived out the roughest years of his young life. And yet it had been a haven, a safe place in his upended world.

"I didn't think it would go down so far so fast," he said softly.

"We've had some rough weather. But I should have thought about keeping an eye on it, after she passed."

Jamie glanced at True. "It wasn't your job."

"She was like family to us, too." True smiled sadly. "She was always one of the few people I could count on for the truth, about what it was going to be like. That there'd be no getting over this, only through it."

Jamie nodded as they walked toward the house. "She knew. She'd been there even before my folks died."

"Who? Did you ever find out?" True asked as they came to a halt in the front yard.

"She never talked about it much, but I found some photos once, of a guy in uniform. Camo stuff. She found me looking at them. I asked her who it was, and she said 'My heart.'"

True winced, and Jamie nodded. Not wanting to dwell on it, he turned his attention back to the house. "I guess I'm lucky no one broke in and trashed the place."

True made an odd sound. "Uh…someone did. Not trash it, but…broke in."

He was surprised at how that jabbed at him. "What? When?"

"A while back." True grimaced. "Hope."

Jamie blinked. "What?"

"This is where I found her."

Now he was staring. "You found Hope in my aunt's house?"

True sighed. "It's a long story. She was desperate. Needed shelter. And she didn't damage anything, really, just a window, and—"

Jamie held up a hand. "I wouldn't care if she had. Especially now that I've met her. And seen the change she's made in you."

True shrugged again, but he was smiling. "Best day of my life was when she hit me with Aunt Millie's mop."

Jamie laughed out loud. The first time he had in a long time, he realized. And he dared to hope that he might truly find what he needed, back here. Here, where he'd once before pieced his shattered life back together, with the help of his loving aunt and an equally shattered girl with huge blue eyes.

Maybe returning to the beginning really was the only way to go on.

Chapter Seven

"WELL, WHAT DO you know?" Zee said. "I couldn't believe it when my brother told me you were here and actually working."

Jamie, who had gone still when she'd begun to speak, slowly straightened from the pile of debris he'd been stacking more neatly beside Millie's house. He'd worked up a sweat in the late spring heat, and his T-shirt was damp with it. Damp and clingy, she noted sourly. Even needing another ten pounds on him, the guy was built. Damn him.

"It's been known to happen," he said, and she knew he must have worked at the neutral tone. She tried to match it.

"You're going to need a shower."

"True got the power turned on, and the well pump still works, so I'm good." He grimaced. "As soon as I clean the bathroom a little."

"I brought the things you told True you wanted. He's kind of busy at the moment."

"I know. Deck and Kelsey's wedding."

"Have you seen them yet?" He and Declan had quite hit

it off when they'd all banded together to be Hope's backup in L.A., discovering that each was a fan of the other's work.

He shook his head. "But I talked to Deck a while ago."

"So they know you're here."

"Yes."

"But you don't want anyone else to."

"Not yet. If I can help it."

"Why?" She was genuinely curious.

"People get weird," he said with a wry grimace. "And I need some time."

Alone.

He didn't say the word, but she heard it as clearly as if he had. "I see." She tried to stop herself from going on, but couldn't. "Tell me, if you hadn't needed True, would I even know you were here?"

He drew back sharply. "Zee—"

"Never mind. Sorry. Swore I wasn't going there." She looked around the neglected property, at the debris he'd stacked. Held up one of the shopping bags. "What's with the sleeping bag?"

He let her change the subject. "Temporary solution. Until I get things into shape." His mouth quirked wryly. "Well, True and I. When he's got time."

She hesitated, drew in a breath, then asked, "So…you're staying for a while?"

"Isn't that what you wanted me to do? Take care of Millie's place?"

"Me? How about her? She loved this place, and you enough to leave it to you. How could you not see to it?"

"I am."

"Finally. Nearly three years after she died."

He was starting to look harassed now. "I didn't realize there was a set timetable."

"I just don't understand how—" She heard her own voice rising, knew she was slipping the leash she'd been determined to keep tight. How could he still do this to her, after all this time? "Never mind," she said again, and then asked the question she didn't want to ask but—for some reason she didn't want to acknowledge—needed to know the answer to. "Cleaning it up to sell?"

He looked suddenly weary again, and she remembered the hollow-eyed man who'd gotten off that plane. "If all you're going to do is snipe at me, just drop the stuff and go, will you?"

She blinked. "That was a simple question."

"Born of your conviction that I hate it here."

"You don't love it. Not like I do." *Not like you say you do, in your music.* Music that still managed to pull at her heart, even knowing it was a lie. She pulled herself away from the thoughts before she voiced them.

"What the hell do you want from me, Zee? What do you expect me to do?"

"The same thing I've always expected. Not to forget where you came from."

"I could never forget that."

"Only how to get here?" He let out a long breath. She took one in. And said for the third time, "I'm sorry. You're hurting over your friend. I shouldn't be chewing on you right now."

"But you reserve the right to tear into me later, is that it?"

He sounded more exasperated than angry, so she risked a small smile. "Something like that."

He looked at her for a long moment, something softer coming into his eyes. "We always did know how to push each other's buttons, didn't we?"

"Yes. Yes, we did." She gestured with the two bags she held and half turned toward the house. "I'll just set these inside."

"Leave the sleeping bag out here, thanks."

She stopped. Glanced back at him. "Is the house so bad you have to sleep outside?"

She was on the verge of telling him to come back to their place, despite the fact that she'd be on edge the entire time, when he blasted that thought right out of her head.

"I'm going to sleep in the tree house."

She froze. "What?"

He gave a one-shouldered shrug. As if it meant nothing. "It's actually in better shape, and it cleaned up fast, so I'll sleep there for a while. And hope the bugs don't carry me off."

She stared at him. He was going to sleep in the tree house. That blessed tree house, where they had first given in to hormones and attraction running hot. After everything, he was going to sleep up there. As if there were no memories at all attached to it.

"Bugs," she muttered. "That's what you're thinking about?"

"It's one of my favorite places." She was sure her emotions must be showing in her face. And a moment later she knew it, because he said softly, "And that's the difference, Zee. You hate the memories from that tree house. I treasure them."

Those memories were about to swamp her, and it put an edge back in her voice. "I don't hate them," she said. "I'm just surprised they matter to you at all."

"Zinnia Rose Mahan, you have no idea what matters to me anymore."

She blinked at his use of her full name. "You're probably right. How could I, when I don't even know who you are anymore?"

"That's okay," he said, suddenly sounding unutterably weary. "Neither do I."

He picked up the sack with the sleeping bag, turned around and headed for the big post oak, leaving her staring after him.

When she got back home, True was in the office labeling some receipts, a habit he'd developed a bit late in the career neither of them had quite realized they had until well into it. That had resulted in a ton of confused paperwork, but it had also resulted in him hiring Hope to straighten it out, and look where that had ended.

It occurred to her to wonder why she'd ended up dropping Jamie's stuff off when her brother was here instead of out at Deck and Kelsey's place, but she let that go in favor of a more pressing question.

"You'll be helping him, right?" she said without preamble.

True lifted a brow at her. "When I can, yes. Why?"

"Just want to be sure he won't always be alone out there."

"Why?" her brother repeated. "He's a big boy, he can take care of himself."

"Can he?" she asked. "He's really off balance right now, hurting, and like you said, rattled."

"Thought you were going to chew on him a bit and bring him back to reality."

I did. Even though I didn't mean to.

"His friend did just die. It's obvious it's really shaken him." She tossed down the handful of receipts he'd just given her. "But maybe that's not a bad thing. I've always been afraid he'd follow that same path."

True's brow furrowed. "Jamie? I think you're underestimating him a bit."

"I think you're underestimating the pull and power of

that world he's living in now. I'd hate to see him end up the same way, even if I am mad at him half the time."

"Anger," True said in his most careful tone, "is still caring."

She watched her brother go, his last words echoing in her head. She supposed he was right. You didn't get angry if you didn't care. But it wasn't love. Not anymore.

You hate the memories from that tree house. I treasure them.

She would have sworn on her life he meant those words. It had been in his voice, in his eyes when he'd said them.

But if it were really true, in the way it should be true—the way she'd once so wanted them to be true—Jamie Templeton would have come back home a long time ago.

And back to her.

THIS WAS THE farthest of far cries from his canyon house in L.A., Jamie thought as he lay staring up at the rough-hewn roof of the tree house. He shifted slightly, grateful True had thought of the air mattress he hadn't. But then that was True. Tell him what you wanted the result to be, and he'd give you a plan and a list of materials off the top of his head and he'd be right down to the last nail.

He was on top of the sleeping bag, risking whatever bugs might make it up here and through the holes in the screens, because the heat of the day had lingered into twilight. He thought in a while he might actually try to sleep, even after last night, when he'd crashed so hard at True's that he hadn't quite been able to believe what time it was when he'd finally awakened.

He almost regretted it, because now his brain was rested enough to run wild. It naturally went to last week, to the hours spent waiting to hear what he'd already known in his gut—Derek was dead. From there to his colliding reactions, horror that it had happened, almost overpowered by the guilt he felt for not noticing in time just how out of it the guy was, and for feeling awful, but not quite as bad as he thought he should, not as bad as he would have had it been one of the others. Logic argued that he'd known them for years and Derek for only a few months, but logic didn't always play into emotion.

From there he'd let his mind loose, and it was doing its usual bounce around from one thing to another, yet shying away from the big, looming thing. He looked at the planks of the tree house roof and remembered True helping him one summer. Not building it—he'd wanted to do that himself—but making suggestions he'd been, even at fifteen, smart enough to heed.

He'd have to redo some of the screening; there were a couple of rips here and there. The rolls of fine mesh had been True's idea, too, in case he wanted to be out here at the height of mosquito season. He'd already repaired rungs of the rope ladder, which True had also wisely suggested he make from nylon rather than natural fiber; it had endured where the other would likely be rotted by now.

"Just be careful," he'd said. "It's pretty elastic so if it breaks, the snapback could do some damage."

The warning had only added spice to the adventure.

His mind slid then into wondering if True and Hope were planning on having kids. True would make a great dad. Hadn't he already practically raised two, him and Zee?

No, not going back to Zee, brain. Especially not here.

He shifted position, his arm nudging the guitar, still in the case that lay beside him.

Oh, no. Definitely not going there, either.

He wasn't even sure why he'd brought the thing up here, except it had felt wrong to leave it in the house alone. His mouth twisted wryly. He was thinking as if it were still alive, still that willing, wonderful partner, helping him make those emotions into music. As if it were still that instrument that had led him from this very tree house to the bright lights and thin air of success.

Something caught his eye, something on the edge of his vision. He sat up to look through the mesh. A tiny flash of light. Then another.

He'd been gone so long it took him a moment.

Fireflies.

The moment he realized the air seemed full of them, flitting, circling, dashing, painting the air with their golden lights. The gift of spring rains, Aunt Millie had called them.

She had loved these shows, and would watch as long as they lasted. He'd made up a song for her about them, one that had made her laugh and sing along with him. That had been the first time he'd really felt not whole, but mended, since the crash that had taken his parents.

Thank you, Aunt Millie.

For what, sweetie?

For everything.

You've given me much more than you've taken, so I should be thanking you.

Pain tightened his chest. He stared at the darting lights, aching with the memories, all of them, his parents, Aunt Millie, now Derek...and the part of himself that was now gone just as completely. Maybe he'd had to come back here, to where it began, to finally face it.

Once, he would have reached for the guitar, to make up some darting, buoyant tune that matched the flight of those little specks of light. But that was pointless now. A useless thought. Because he knew all the speculation that the death of his friend was the beginning of something, of a reassessment, a reorienting, and that he would be back after a suitable period, was wrong.

Derek's death hadn't been the beginning. It had been the culmination of a process that had begun some time ago. The process he'd at last admitted to, sitting on the floor of an emergency room waiting area, and only finally faced at the funeral.

Derek's death, aside from the heartbreak of it, didn't

mark the start of anything.

It marked the end.

It marked Jamie Templeton's final admission of the truth.

The music was gone.

Chapter Eight

"HAVE YOU SEEN Jamie?" Deck asked.

"Not since Wednesday," Zee said. "He made it pretty clear he didn't want...company." *Me.*

She'd tried to keep her tone level, but apparently she hadn't succeeded, because he said, rather carefully, "You're like Kels. If she's hurting, she turns to family, friends."

She frowned. "Of course. Who else would you turn to?"

Deck gave her a wry half-smile. "Me, I want to go hole up somewhere alone until I chew my way through it."

"But you need people—"

"Some do," he cut her off, but quietly. "Some of us...it's better if we're alone until we can at least see the other side."

She studied him for a moment. Remembered the old stories about Crazy Joe, the recluse. Realized she was witnessing a small miracle, Deck reaching out like this, being so open. Maybe it was simply because he'd come to trust True completely, and it had stretched to include his sister. Whatever it was, she appreciated it.

"I didn't think of it like that," she admitted.

"It doesn't mean we care any less, that we hurt any less. We just handle it differently." His mouth quirked. "And run into a lot of people who think our way is wrong and theirs right."

"Like me?"

"Like most people," he said tactfully, then dropped it. "True tells me you know Jamie better than anyone."

Zee managed to fight down the heat that wanted to flood her cheeks. For she had spent most of the night thinking about just how well she knew Jamie Templeton, from the quirky workings of his brilliant mind to every gorgeous inch of his body. What little sleep she'd gotten had been no respite, for then the dreams had come, dreams of heated moments in a tree house and then, even worse, dreams of here and now, of finding out if he still liked that little nibble on his ear, if a sliding touch inward from his hipbone still made him shiver.

And in those dreams, of course he'd forgotten none of what drove her mad, the things she'd learned about herself from their exuberant explorations. He'd been the same careful, generous, impossibly sexy lover he'd been until the day he'd walked out of Whiskey River and her life.

Like he'd remember. All those women, groupies at his beck and call—why would he remember what that silly girl back home liked?

She schooled her expression to calm, although she didn't know if it would be enough to fool the very perceptive

Declan Kilcoyne. And whatever he was after, it had to be important, for him to steal time away from his work and his beloved Kelsey this close to their wedding and come practically into town to her door.

"We spent a lot of time together," she said. "Only natural, after our parents were killed in the same accident."

Deck didn't waste breath on condolences for the long-ago tragedy, and she was grateful for that. She knew he had no idea what it would have felt like, to even have loving parents let alone lose them, and she appreciated that he didn't pretend he did.

"Is he different, now? I don't mean just grief over his friend, I mean...something deeper?"

Her eyes widened. She'd started to wonder if she'd been imagining something beyond grief at the death of a friend, but if Deck had seen it, too...

It still took her aback, that she was standing here talking to one of the most famous authors in the world, as if he were any other friend. And he was a friend, no longer just the reclusive client who had helped begin Mahan Services. And because of that, she could not, would not do what she might with someone else, dodge his question. And if Deck cared enough to ask, he deserved a straight answer.

"I don't know what it is, but I sense it, too."

After a moment Deck nodded. "I guess we'll just have to keep a close eye on him, then."

Zee smiled, diverted for the moment. "And you're the

guy who once said you didn't know a thing about being a friend."

"I didn't," Deck said. Then he smiled, that flashing, brilliant smile that Kelsey had given him. "But I've had a great teacher."

"And now you've got friends who'd go to the mat for you."

He actually flushed. "Yeah. How about that?"

And there, she thought after he'd gone, was another one who wouldn't understand her anger. She wasn't sure she understood it herself anymore.

Being Zee, she resorted to her go-to…she made a list. She sat at her desk, pulled over a note pad. Wrote "MAD" in caps across the top, then drew a line down the center of a blank page. Down the left side she listed all the reasons she could think of that made her angry with Jamie, even if down deep she knew they were unfair. Down the right, she wrote what she guessed was his side of it. And then she sat back and studied the columns.

He never came back/They hit it big, momentum

Not even to see to Aunt Millie's things/But he was there for her when she got ill

Across both columns, As Deck said, different ways of processing?

Sex, drugs, and rock and roll?/Less than most, maybe. ← As if that's an excuse!

Hypocrite, sings about home but never even visits/But he remembers, it shows

Thinks he's too big for us now?/Went over and above when True needed him

Said he loved me but left anyway/Never lied about it, he was always going to

Her gaze snagged on that last one. She knew it was the hardest for her, even though of all of them, it was the most unfair.

Be sure, Zee. Because I'm still leaving. We're heading west as soon as we can and I don't know when we'll be back.

When. Not if. Like the foolish girl she'd been, she'd clung to that word.

She'd just never expected it to be once in seven years, and driven by death, not love.

And now? Driven by death again.

She threw her pen down on the pad. It rolled, until it covered that last line. She reached to move it, then stopped. What if she left it? What if she took that last line out of the equation? The unfair one, the one she knew deep down she didn't really have any right to?

He had never lied to her. He'd warned her, time and again. It was not his fault if her heart had been silly enough to think that things would change, after what they'd found together. That was hers to own, not his to carry.

She read the rest of the list again. And finally admitted that, were it not for that last line, everything on that list was…forgivable. And would have been forgiven in a friend long ago.

It was only that he'd been her lover that tilted the balance. And she'd just admitted that was the one complaint that was most unfair. And she had the uncomfortable feeling she'd been clinging to that hurt like the teenager she'd been, long after she should have let it go. They'd had almost three years together, although the last two were as much apart as together as the band began to tour locally, taking any gig offered in the effort to get themselves out there.

But he'd always come home, then. And she foolishly had thought it would continue that way as their reach expanded. And then the chance at L.A. had appeared, the chance to open for a big-name band at a string of West Coast dates. She'd expected him to go—you didn't turn down a chance like that.

She just hadn't expected that he'd never come back.

Time to grow up, Zinnia Rose.

She only used that name even in her thoughts when she was being the most stern with herself. And she'd apparently decided she deserved that just now. The question was, what now?

That was going to take some more thought.

Chapter Nine

"You're working pretty hard for a Sunday morning."

Jamie dropped the bag of yard debris he'd collected and spun around.

"Zee."

"And you're awake, too," she said lightly, and with a smile. For a moment he just looked at her warily. "I brought a peace offering."

She opened the top of the white bag she carried, then held it out toward him. He got a whiff of the aroma.

His eyes widened. "Cinnamon rolls?"

"Straight from the bakery. Still warm." His stomach growled so loudly she heard it. And laughed. "Guess that answers that."

He nearly shivered despite the warmth of the sun in a clear blue sky. He hadn't heard that laugh, a genuine laugh, from her in so long he wasn't sure how to read it. But it hadn't seemed fake or forced.

"I brought coffee, too," she said. "I didn't know what

you had here."

"Um…nothing?"

She blinked. "What have you been eating? And if you say nothing, I may rethink this peace offering," she added sternly.

He suddenly remembered something True had often said: Never get in the way of a determined Zee Mahan.

"No, I've eaten," he said quickly, his eye still on that bag giving off the tempting smell. "Hope dropped off some stuff, and Deck brought a bag of fast food yesterday. I ate it all."

"Well, I'd give you the eat healthy lecture, but you know I'm as bad as you are about it, so I won't."

He smiled at that as he took the bag. Looked inside. "Wow. Half a dozen? I'll keel over in a sugar coma."

"I thought you might share. In the nature of tipping the delivery person."

His gaze shot back to her face. This was almost the old Zee, the gently teasing Zee rather than the one looking daggers at him all the time. God, he'd missed her.

"I gave you three days," she said softly. "Now it's time for some company."

"I'd…like that."

He looked around; there was no furniture in the house, or anything else for that matter, he'd cleared it out to the walls and floor this morning. And Millie's old picnic table was long gone, he didn't know where.

"We can sit outside," she said.

"The tree house?" he suggested before he thought.

The barest flicker of tightness flashed across her face, and he wished the words back, for all the good it did.

"Not ready for that," she said, and although her tone was even, he could tell it was an effort. Which he appreciated she was making.

"Sorry," he said. "Down to the river, then? Our rock?"

Another flicker as he mentioned the outcrop of limestone that jutted into the river at the edge of the property, but she nodded.

"All right."

They started walking. The rock had been carved out over the years by occasional floodwaters, until it had an almost bench-like shape to it, where you could sit and dangle your feet in the water. Water moccasin bait, Aunt Millie used to say.

And he and Zee had shared it so many times, since that night that had turned both their lives upside down. She'd cried in his arms, apologizing as she did. He'd asked her once why she kept saying she was sorry, and she'd said she could only do this with him because True had too much to carry already.

"But he's the one crying for the same people you are, Zee," he'd told her then.

His words had reached her, and she and True had drawn even closer. And a few years later, he'd turned those moments into a song, and "Crying Alone" had become one of the band's most enduring hits.

And I feel like crying all over again, for yet another loss.

He shook off the thought as Zee glanced up at the tree house as they passed. Her expression was shuttered, unreadable, even for him.

"I'm sorry," he said.

"For what?"

"A lot of things. But mostly because that place—" he nodded toward the big post oak "—isn't the beautiful memory for you that it is for me."

"Oh."

"Was it really that bad, Zee?" He grimaced at his own words, thinking he shouldn't start this, that her mellow mood wouldn't last if he did, but he was driven to know. "I always thought it was…incredible. Or am I just being a guy and romanticizing my first time?"

She stopped in her tracks. Stared at him. There was no mask now, she was startled. "Your first time?"

He frowned. "Well, ours, but I meant—"

"That was your first time, too?" she clarified, still staring at him.

His frown deepened. "Of course it was."

"But you had girls all over you at school."

He grimaced again. "They never paid any attention to me before the accident. I was just that weird kid to them. After, I guess I suddenly got 'interesting.' Or worse, to be pitied. You think I wanted that?"

"I wouldn't. I didn't. I hated that." She was still staring at him. "Why didn't you tell me then?"

"Because I thought you knew. That you were…my first, too."

"How could I?" She gave him a sideways look. "You were so…good at it."

For a moment he just stared at her. And couldn't help the silly grin that spread across his face. "I was, huh?"

"Quit smirking, or I'm taking back those cinnamon rolls."

And that quickly she was the old Zee again, quick with a comeback and always teasing him. He wasn't certain what had just happened, but it gave him hope.

ZEE SAVORED THE last bite of the second cinnamon roll she'd eaten. She hadn't intended on two, but nothing about this day was going as she'd thought it would.

…you were my first, too.

She'd been wrong. All this time she'd been wrong. She'd assumed he'd already taken that step with one of those popular girls who'd suddenly noticed he was alive, now that he'd become a tragic sort of figure at school. She'd assumed because he had seemed to know every step, every way to kiss her, touch her, to make her tremble, make her ache for him. He'd been gentle yet fierce, and it had been, as he'd said, incredible.

So if it wasn't experience, what had it been? Her seventeen-year-old self would have answered it had been because it was destiny. The self that had done without him ever since had a different opinion, but she didn't want to think about that just now. They'd healed a part of the breach at least today, and she didn't want to jeopardize that.

"You understood, back then, that I needed to share my grief with True."

He gave her a half-shrug that was reminiscent of her brother, and wondered if that's where he picked it up or if it was just a male thing. Like that smirking, self-satisfied grin at his own prowess.

"But you didn't share yours."

"I did, with you. And Aunt Millie. Sometimes."

Her mouth quirked. "And then you went off by yourself and wouldn't let us help you."

"I needed to be by myself. To…process it."

She thought of wise words she'd recently heard. "Deck called it holing up somewhere alone until he could chew through it."

"That's what I felt like," he admitted. "Like I needed to den up like a wounded animal, until I healed." He looked down at the bakery bag his fingers were worrying at. "Or died."

She ached at the familiar words that so well described the feeling she never wanted to experience again. "And instead you turned it into a thing of beauty, a song that touched millions of people."

He smiled, but wryly. "I think you might be overestimating a bit."

"I'm not. Last time I looked, the video for it was up over two and a half million views."

He blinked. "Was it?"

She gave a little laugh. "And that you don't know that is part of your charm, Mr. Head Scorpion."

"I…haven't been keeping track of much lately."

And there it was again, that sensation that there was more going on with him than simply the loss, albeit tragic, of a bandmate who'd been with them only a few months. But she sensed that if she asked, he would avoid answering. Whatever it was, he clearly wasn't ready to talk about it.

So instead she asked, "Do you ever get tired of playing the same songs? The big hits?"

He shrugged. Male thing, she decided. "Those songs are what bought us the ticket for this crazy flight. They're what people want to hear. Besides, it's different live."

She tilted her head to look at him quizzically. "How?"

"The feedback. Instantaneous, from the audience. It fires us up."

She nodded slowly, because that made sense to her. "So…you still like it. The touring, I mean."

"What was it that other Texas boy sang, about the road going on forever, and the party that never ends?"

"A lot of Texas boys have sung that song," she said wryly. "But sometimes the party has to end, so you can clean up the mess."

She hadn't meant it to be a jab, just an observation on the lifestyle, but he went very still. And in that instant she knew, deep in her bones, that she'd been right, that this man who had been the boy she'd adored was battling something more than he'd said.

"Yes," he said after a moment, and his voice was low, harsh. "Sometimes the party has to end."

And it hurt just to see his face, because he looked as bleak, as desolate as he had in the days after both their lives had been ripped apart.

Chapter Ten

IT NEARLY TOOK him down this time. That dark, swirling cloud closed in, and it was all he could do to fight it off. But he had to—he couldn't let it overtake him now, not with Zee sitting right here. Not when they were having the most...not pleasant, but non-antagonistic conversation they'd had in years.

"Jamie," she whispered, and there was an undertone in her voice that told him what must be showing in his face. He fought the cloud, clung to her voice, that voice that had once been the only one he ever wanted to hear.

"You know what I used to think when it got really crazy, when I nearly stepped off the edge?"

"What?"

"I used to think, 'Man, Zee would chew me out for that.' And I stepped back."

She was staring at him, looking almost stunned. "I...I'm glad, then. Surprised, but glad."

"Why surprised?"

"I didn't think you thought of me, or home, at all, once

you were out of here."

"Zee—"

"I didn't mean that as a slam, or an accusation," she said quickly. "And I always knew Whiskey River couldn't hold you."

"But it never let go, either. Ever." He waited a moment, expecting her to ask why, then, he never came home. She was looking at him as if the question were hovering, but she didn't speak the words. Finally, he asked her. "Why are you happy here?"

She gave a puzzled shrug. "It's home."

"You never wanted more?"

She looked toward the river, glistening under the spring sun. "To see? Yes. To stay? Never."

Suddenly the intro riff of "River Song" rang out. It was a bit disconcerting anyway, but when he realized it was the ring tone on her cell, it was even more so.

"Wow," he said rather hurriedly, "a call actually got through out here."

"Yeah." She didn't look at him as she dug the phone out of her pocket. He saw the photo on the screen as she put it to her ear. True.

"I'm out at Millie's," she said into the phone. A pause and then, rather acerbically, "Yes, he's still alive."

Jamie went still. Was her brother teasing her about not killing him? Or did True think he was in worse shape than he was and might do it himself?

He wasn't that deep. Was he?

Not yet.

He clung to those two words as she finished her call, then got to her feet.

"I have to pick up the speakers that just came in. The last of the sound system for the wedding."

He got up himself. "Deck's really doing it up right, isn't he?"

"For a guy who was so near hopeless not that long ago, it's amazing. But he wants the best for Kelsey. And she's smart enough to let him do it."

"Smart enough?" He'd had no doubt Kelsey Blaine was smart—it had been obvious when he'd met her on the Hope flight. But he wasn't sure how it applied to this.

"Deck's never had the chance, or the need, to really give to someone. Kelsey knows how important that is, so she's letting him."

"I...think I get that," he said, giving a slow nod.

"She's a very smart lady. Especially about creatures who are hurting, equine or human."

Deck had told him, with surprising straightforwardness, how close he'd been to the edge before Kelsey had thrown him a lifeline.

Zee looked at him considering for a moment before she said, "You want to come? Give you a chance to see their place. You never got to before, did you?"

"I... No."

Her mouth tightened so slightly he doubted anyone would notice, except someone who had once been attuned to every flicker of emotion in that lovely face.

"No to which? Or was that both?"

"I haven't been there. But you have to go into town to pick up the speakers, don't you?"

"Only to the package pickup out on the highway, outside of town. True told them to hold them there rather than wait for whenever the delivery truck would get there." She gave him a sideways look. "You can hide in the car, Mr. Celebrity. We'll keep you a secret a while longer."

"Look, it's just that—"

"I get it," she said. "But you do know the Whiskey River grapevine is as efficient as ever. Sooner or later it's going to get out that one of our most famous sons is back."

He did know. From personal experience. He just wanted to put it off as long as possible. But the lure of having more of this non-battling conversation with her was too much to deny.

"At least you didn't say infamous," he said.

"That I wouldn't know," she said, "since I try to always follow Aunt Millie's advice."

He grinned at that—he couldn't help it. "Believe half of what you see and none of what you hear?"

She grinned back. "Exactly."

And in that moment they were those two kids again, thrown together by tragedy and finding, to their surprise, a connection they'd never expected. He felt lighter than he had in months.

"You just want me to do the heavy lifting," he said with over-the-top accusation.

"This from the guy who could put the skinny in skinny-dipping right now?" she countered.

Skinny-dipping with Zee. Now that was a scenario with potential.

Whoa. Where the hell had that come from?

He looked away. Fought off the sensations that had rocketed through him on the thought. Focused on gathering up the remnants of the tray of cinnamon rolls they had demolished. "You keep this up," he said, gesturing with the bag without looking at her, "and I'll put on twenty pounds."

"Since you need ten, I'll take the extra."

As long as you take the rest, too.

He bit his lip. It had to be reflex. Just being in this place, back home, was making the old feelings, thoughts and ideas well up again.

The old urges too, apparently.

Since he couldn't think of anything to say that wouldn't get him in deeper, he said nothing as they got in her car. He realized this meant he'd be dependent on her for a ride back, and wondered if he should rent a car. Or even buy one, although that smacked of permanency.

The moment he thought it he felt a twinge. His mind skittered away from it. Like a cockroach away from the light, he thought sourly. Because that's what he did, apparently. Keep people's expectations where you want them, so you don't have to deal with the discomfort of disappointing them. He wondered how much of his life had been ruled by that premise, born of the first time he'd walked away from Whiskey River.

And Zee.

Because he'd known. Oh, she hadn't cried, or wailed at him, or even begged him to stay. It might have been easier if she had. But she hadn't, she'd merely looked at him and nodded. Been cool as could be as they packed up their gear in the old van Boots had driven from Austin, and headed out that last time. She watched them go, calm, accepting...if you didn't look at her eyes.

He'd carried that last glimpse of those devastated blue eyes with him every moment of his life since.

He stayed in the car as she went in to pick up the gear True had ordered, but got out to help as she arrived with a large flatbed dolly. The four big boxes wouldn't fit in the trunk, so they put two in, then the other two in the backseat. The businesslike discussion of how to arrange them was the first time they'd spoken since leaving Millie's. And the silence settled in again when, cargo secured, she pulled out of the lot and headed back north.

It wasn't all that far from Aunt Millie's to Deck's place, he thought. He could walk back. He knew that because everybody knew where the place they dubbed the castle—for the big stone turret that overlooked the river—was. As a kid, he and his friend Antonio had even snuck out there once. That was when it was standing empty, a monument to whimsy, and long before a certain recluse of a writer moved in.

They'd done it on bikes, and it hadn't seemed far at all.

Does anything when you've got the energy of a twelve-year-old?

His mom hadn't been happy when she'd found out. She went into her "What if you'd gotten hurt?" lecture. He had, wisely for once, stayed quiet, but that wasn't because he'd suddenly gotten smart, it was because he was trying to figure out how the hell she'd found out.

He and Antonio had finally pieced it all together; how the mailman had seen them headed north in town, then one of the Kellys had seen them leaving the city limits, and finally old man Roper who owned the land next to the castle, where Kelsey's rescue now was, now had spotted them going by. It had been his first personal experience with the Whiskey River grapevine, which was nothing if not efficient.

And two years later his loving, worried mother was gone, never again to hug him close even as she lectured him.

In that instant, the grief hit him all over again. It was as powerful, as fierce as it had ever been. For that moment he was that fourteen-year-old boy, remembering True's girl Amanda arriving with Aunt Millie to break the news, with a broken, sobbing Zee in tow.

He didn't think he'd made a sound, but Zee looked over at him. And frowned. In a worried, not an angry way. "Jamie?"

He sucked in a breath. The pain receded. He'd come to believe the only thing anyone ever gained was that moments like this were fewer, farther between. But when they came, it was as if it had been yesterday.

"Sorry," he muttered, guessing what he must have looked like. "I just...slipped back to that day. The accident."

Zee looked back at the road. And then she sang softly, "'There is a way to time travel, just lose someone you love.'"

He went still. "Time Travel." It wasn't one of their big hits, probably because he couldn't bear to sing it very often, so it was rarely on their set list. But their rabid fans had found it, embraced it, so the video had a ton of views, and it had been downloaded so often he'd lost track of the number.

"You gave so many people help with that song," Zee said. "Including me."

"Most people assume it's about the end of a love affair," he said, his voice rough.

"I know. But the first time I heard it I knew it was really about much more."

"I knew you would. If anyone would, you would."

They might have lost everything else they'd had, but they would never lose two things. They had that terrible common bond of being orphaned in the same instant. And Zee was the one who ever and always understood the music.

He almost told her. It almost spilled out, right there in the car. Because she was the one who always understood. But he couldn't. He couldn't, because putting it into words, especially to her, would make it real.

And he wasn't at all sure he could live with that particular reality.

Chapter Eleven

THE MINUTE HE saw Kelsey and Deck he was glad he'd come. Even if they were wrapped tight in a lip-lock that had him wondering how they were breathing.

"God, they make my heart ache. In a good way," Zee said as she pulled the car up next to the pavilion True had built for them. She gave him a sideways look and added, "And if you ever tell them I said that I'll never bring you another cinnamon roll."

"Can't have that," he said, feeling another spark of gladness at this bit of the old, teasing Zee back again. "But is it okay if I say they make me feel the same way?"

When she'd shut off the car she looked at him. "It would even more if you'd seen the way he was before Kelsey. When True first started to work for him."

"He told me some. I kind of guessed at the rest. I'd already read some of his books."

Finally coming up for air, Kelsey spotted them then, and waved as they started toward Zee's car. They both looked a little surprised when he got out, but then he was engulfed in two simultaneous hugs. There was a lot of chatter for a couple of minutes, and he would have felt overwhelmed had it not been so genuinely delighted.

"Sorry about your friend," Deck said.

"Yeah." He couldn't think of another word at the moment.

"Talk about it or not. We're good," Kelsey said.

He felt a burst of relief at their willingness to let it be. Then realized that everyone standing here knew up close and personal about loss. "Hell of a club we all belong to, isn't it?"

"You mean the one no one wants to join, but almost everyone eventually does?" Zee said.

"Yeah."

"Sucks."

"In a word," Deck agreed.

Then, briskly, Zee said, "We brought your speakers."

Everyone seemed glad of the change of subject. Jamie knew he was.

"Great," Deck said, "that's about the final piece. Just need True to get them hooked up."

Jamie glanced at the pavilion. "He's already got it wired?"

"And power run out to it. You know True. Down to the last detail," Kelsey said.

"Yeah," Jamie agreed. He hesitated, then said, "I know those speakers. And sound stuff generally. I could hook them up right now, if you want." His mouth quirked. "And if you trust me."

"That would be great," Deck exclaimed.

"And save True yet another trip," Kelsey added.

"You say that now," Zee said. "Wait until you see his bill."

Jamie shot her a glance, saw nothing but her old, teasing grin. He breathed again. When he looked back Kelsey and Deck were exchanging a rather pointed glance, but he didn't ask.

They walked over to the pavilion. It was, as he expected, built solid. Big, but not overpowering, and he noticed the concrete foundation was curved with the same arc of the river beyond, which it was angled to face. The crossbeams were sturdy, yet the ends had been neatly cut in an echoing curve, and the edges were trimmed with stone that looked remarkably like the stone of the tower, making it seem as if it truly belonged. All the attention to detail that was a True Mahan trademark.

With Deck helping, he had the four speakers up in the racks True had built in just a few minutes. Connecting them should only take a bit longer, he thought.

"Great spot," he said from atop the ladder as he finished the last one. "It's going to be a heck of a wedding."

"Still won't be good enough for her," Deck said solemnly. "Nothing could be."

Jamie looked down at the man who had, so unexpectedly, become a good friend. "I envy you." Then, with a wry grimace added, "But not what you went through to get here."

Deck smiled, and it held only a touch of sad reminiscence. "I try to look on it now only as material for Sam."

Jamie slowly smiled back. "I get that."

"I thought you would."

Jamie had the feeling the man wanted to say more, but when he didn't, he went back to work. It had been a while, but when Scorpions had started out, they'd been running on a shoestring and had done it all themselves. Things had changed a bit, but the basics were the basics, and they'd had these same speakers at the last outdoor venue they'd played, albeit a bigger version.

He finished the last connection then went down the ladder. "We'd better test it, make sure I haven't forgotten the days when we used to hook up our own sound."

"Yeah," Deck said. He glanced toward the river, where Kelsey and Zee where standing, talking animatedly. Then he took a deep breath. But still didn't speak.

"Whatever it is that's hovering, just say it," Jamie suggested.

"Kels and I…we…look, we'll understand if you don't want to do the song. At the wedding."

Jamie's breath caught. He'd been a bit taken aback when they'd first asked him. Not that they'd asked, he was pleased by that, but that Kelsey had said she wanted him to sing "Morning" right after she walked down the aisle, as part of the ceremony, not just the reception after. He hadn't even realized she listened to them, she'd been so discreet. When she said it had been one of her favorite songs since it had come out, and that it had special significance to her and Deck, he'd been surprised at how that made him feel.

And that they were tactfully giving him the chance to back out now, at this late date, told him the immediate connection he'd felt with this couple was real. They were more worried about him than the biggest day of their lives together. And he couldn't find words to say how that made him feel, so he tried turning it around.

"Change your mind?" he asked, keeping his tone light. "I get it, been a bit of bad press lately."

Deck looked utterly shocked. "What?"

"Drug OD, lots of headlines. Might not be the kind of thing you want attached to your wedding."

Jamie had had a lot of practice reading people's reactions, since so often with him they were over-the-top. But he knew when Deck's expression changed that this was real.

"I should knock you on your celebrated ass for even thinking that."

And he could probably do it, Jamie thought. There was still enough of the fighter who had survived things no kid should ever have to deal with in this guy. "Back at you," he said softly, "for thinking I'd want to back out."

Deck got it. Nodded. "Just wanted to give you the chance."

"Yeah. Thanks for that. But I wouldn't miss it." He grinned suddenly. "But just remember I told you I've never sung at a wedding before."

"I do." Deck grinned back. "Been thinking we should sell tickets. We could raise a lot for Kelsey's rescue."

Jamie lifted a brow at him. "They need it?"

Deck sighed. "She's a little…stubborn. About taking money for it."

"From you, you mean."

"It's not some hobby to her, it's a calling. Besides, she says it makes people feel good to help, and she doesn't want to take that away from them."

Jamie glanced over to where the two women were walking back toward them. "You're a lucky man, my friend."

"Yes." Then, after a moment. "So, should we not put you and Zee at the same table?"

Startled, Jamie's gaze shot back to Deck. "I…"

Deck shrugged. "Hard to miss there was a bit of an edge there."

"Especially for an observer like you," Jamie said wryly.

"It's what I do," Deck agreed.

Kelsey and Zee were within earshot now, so he said only, "I'll let you know."

And he tried to take heart in the fact that, even three days ago, the answer would have been, "Different tables."

Chapter Twelve

"Where are you staying?" Kelsey asked as she reached for another chip.

"At my aunt's place," Jamie said, wiping his fingers after the last bite of what had been a rather amazingly good roast beef sandwich. He'd missed the way Texans let the meat speak for itself, with only the simplest of flavorings, not the elaborate sauces and trendy sides that L.A. seemed prone to.

They were gathered in the kitchen, which Jamie had to say was one of the most unique kitchens he'd ever seen. "It's kind of overwhelming at first, three different kinds of stone and the dramatic grain of the hickory cabinets, but it's growing on me," Kelsey had said.

"What he means by his aunt's place," Zee said, her tone dry but not acerbic, "is he's living in the tree house."

"The tree house?" Kelsey said, clearly startled.

But Deck only leaned back in his chair at the table and nodded. "That's really getting back to the beginning."

Zee looked suddenly thoughtful. "I hadn't thought of it quite like that." She shifted her gaze back to Jamie. "Is that it?"

"Partly."

"I thought you were just...doing your loner thing."

"That, too."

"Take it from an expert," Deck said, "he's got a ways to go on that."

Kelsey laughed. "And you are an expert."

"Was."

"That, too," Kelsey agreed blithely.

After lunch Jamie went back outside and headed toward the river, curious to see it from here, see how different it might be from where it flowed shallowly past Aunt Millie's.

Except it's not Aunt Millie's anymore. It's yours.

He swatted at the thought as if it were a Texas-sized mosquito. Focused on the water. It was deeper here, so smoother on top except where it divided to pass an outcropping of stone. He knew they had about a hundred acres here, and in that moment he envied that. Wondered if there was enough in his personal kitty to buy something like this. He hadn't paid enough attention to that—

"Mind an interruption?"

He nearly jumped; he hadn't heard Kelsey approach. And saying he minded didn't really occur to him; he was standing on essentially her property. Because there was no doubt in his mind that she and Declan Kilcoyne were a united front—those two had definitely become one.

"Your place is really great."

"It's got…character."

He smiled at her. "That's what they say when they've got a house that's so unique it might only fit one person."

She grinned. "And this one fits Deck."

"What about you?"

"It's a bit big," she said. "But compared to my old place, a garage was bigger."

He laughed; he'd heard about her falling-down old cabin from True, who had been in charge of mowing it down. Which had been the spark that had started the fire that was Kelsey and Deck.

"I wanted to ask," she said, "about you and Zee."

He drew back slightly. "Whoa. That's jumping right into the fire."

"I don't know the full history between you two, so I should probably butt out." She paused. He couldn't think of a damned thing to say. "This is where you say 'Yes, you should.' And I walk away, no offense taken."

He studied her for a moment. Kelsey had only come to her father's hometown after he'd already gone, so he didn't know her any better than he knew Deck. But he'd learned a lot back in the spring, watching her—and her dynamic mother—help as Hope took her life back.

"After what you've done for Deck, I'm not sure I should say no to your…advice."

She looked relieved, and smiled. "No advice. Just a female point of view, maybe?"

He had, in fact, had no shortage of that in the last few years. But most of them were telling him why, to use a Texas term, he should cut them out of the herd. He knew that was a terrible way to think about it, but half the time he wanted to ask those women what they were thinking—they didn't know anything about him. He was thankful there had been just as many who weren't interested in that, who were there for the music. And he'd enjoyed just talking with them more than any of the few times his mood had been such that he took one of the other offerings.

He'd expected her to take his silence as assent, but Kelsey simply waited. And he remembered again he was dealing with the woman who had drawn out one of the most reclusive men in the country. He was beginning to see how she'd done it.

"You going to say what you want to say?" It came out a bit edgy, but she never blinked.

"You going to get mad if I do?"

He sighed. "No. Yes. Maybe." She smiled, and he added, "But not at you."

"All I ask. I've gotten to know Zee fairly well. And I know you and Zee were together, up until you hit the road."

The old mantra leapt to his lips. "I never lied to her." He took a breath and went on. "She always knew I was leaving. Hell, she encouraged it, told me to go, to chase the dream."

"Before or after you had sex?"

He blinked. Had she really asked that? And so casually?

When he didn't answer, she went on. "I was a teenage girl once."

"Figured that out."

She ignored his wry comment. "Just like with guys, sometimes the brain is at odds with the heart. And the hormones."

"Remember it well."

"Sometimes the brain is saying one thing, while the heart is screaming 'I don't mean it.'"

"You're saying...she didn't mean it when she said I should go?"

"I mean teenage girls are often conflicted. And when you throw great sex into the mix, it messes it up even more."

His mouth quirked—he couldn't help it. "You're assuming it was great."

"Of course it was, or it would be long forgotten by now. And she wouldn't be driving a car almost the exact color of your eyes."

He stared at her. "Her...car?"

"Hadn't you noticed?"

"I...no."

"I did, the moment I saw you and her car at Devil's Rock that day for Hope's flight."

Did women always notice things like that, tiny details of color and correlation? he wondered. Then again, he'd met her mom, who noticed everything. Maybe it was inherited.

"You're pretty young to be so...wise."

"You've met my mother," she said simply, echoing his own thought. "Look, I'm only saying girls that age can be…stupid. Born romantics that we are."

"Born?"

"Until life beats it out of us, I think most of us are, yes. And even though you never lied to her, maybe her heart still cherished hopes."

"Hopes?"

"That you'd stay with her. That she was that important to you."

He frowned this time. "She was that important. But she was the one who kept pushing me to go for the dream."

"As I said, conflicted."

His mouth twisted. "I think I'd use the word confusing. Maybe baffling."

"No denial here. At that age, we even confuse ourselves. I'm just saying that while she loved you enough to want you to have your dream, and to let you go after it without trying to hold you back, she also loved you so much she wanted you to stay with her."

"I asked her to go with me."

"And to some I'm sure that would be a dream come true. But Zee's a hometown girl. She loves this place. It's her life. And she and her brother are close, and were especially close then. She knows how much she owes him."

"I know." He thought about it for a minute. Maybe longer. Then said slowly, "That's still a long time to stay mad."

"It is, so you're going to have to ask her about now. I was just trying to help with then."

And she had, Jamie acknowledged as they made their way back to the house. For all his thoughts of Zee—and they'd been frequent—he'd never quite looked at their parting like that.

"Kelsey?" he said as they got to the house. She looked at him. "Thanks."

She smiled, and he felt a flash of gladness that she and Deck had found each other.

Kelsey and Deck, True and Hope. He'd bet on them all to endure. He'd bet that decades from now they'd still be together.

But he'd bet even more that he'd still be alone. Or settled for something considerably less than what his friends had gained.

Maybe he'd end as some worn-out rocker riding on past glory. Or maybe not. He wondered how long a four-year ride at the top got you in people's memories.

Or maybe, he thought, trying to chivvy himself out of this sudden pool of self-pity, *you'll just end up as crazy old man Templeton, singing to himself in a tree house.*

Chapter Thirteen

ZEE STOPPED THE car at the end of Deck's long, meandering driveway, waiting for the gate to slide open. And couldn't quite suppress a sigh.

"The happiness fairly rolls off of them, doesn't it?" She heard the almost wistful note in her own voice, didn't like that it was there, but couldn't seem to help it.

"It's obvious they're crazy about each other," Jamie said.

"It would be nauseatingly saccharine if I didn't like them so much."

"And if you weren't aware of what they had to fight to get to here."

"Yes." Zee edged the car through the gate and out to where she could see both directions. Then she glanced at him. "Back to Millie's?"

"Yes. Please."

She wondered if she—or he—would ever start to think of it as his place.

She was pulling into the drive of Aunt Millie's place before he spoke again.

"Zee?"

She didn't shut off the engine, because she had no intention of staying any longer than it took to let him out. She knew he would get it. He was many things, but he was not stupid.

"What?"

"If Deck and Kelsey could get to where they are…"

Her breath jammed up in her throat in that way she hated. The way that made it seem as if she'd never take another easy breath. That way that only he seemed able to do to her.

"…do you think we could at least get back to being friends?"

Friends. Of course. She should have known. And she was an idiot—no, worse than an idiot—to think he'd meant anything else. To think, even for an instant, that he might want to go back to what they'd once been to each other. To become again those soul-deep partners in life, the ones who held each other's secrets, dreams, and hearts. She wasn't sure she wanted that herself.

She went still inside. Of course she didn't. That was over and done. He clearly was no longer the boy who'd left her in the Whiskey River dust, no longer the boy she'd loved so fiercely. No, Jamie Templeton was now far beyond the likes of a small-town girl like her.

And she'd better not forget that, not even for a moment. Even thinking about it opened her up to too much hurt.

"True's who you really need to stay friends with."

She hadn't meant it to sound so sharp. He didn't wince physically, but she saw it in his eyes. Those green eyes that had always so captivated her, even when they'd been full of grief that first night when they'd been huddled together, trying to process the news that their lives as they'd known them were over.

"Damn it, Zee," he said, his voice harsh. "I want to stay here, at least for a while, but I can't do it if you hate me."

She wondered what "a while" constituted in the mind of a guy who was accustomed to hitting a new venue in a new town every night. "I don't. Besides, you don't even have to see me."

"I only have to work with your brother, and worry about running into you at any moment and getting another blast of temper—"

"That's what you think this is?" She stared at him, the old anger rising. That it proved him somewhat right at least did not escape her, but she couldn't seem to help it. "That I'm just in a snit?"

"I don't know what it is," he said, sounding so tired contrition flooded her. Why did she keep breaking her internal promise not to do this? Not now, while he was in this state. "So why don't you tell me? What the hell is this really about? Are you still mad because I left, even after you told me—hell, ordered me to go?"

It sounded so juvenile when he put it like that. So teenage girl. Which is what she'd been, true, but that was then and now was now. But if he wanted to get this out in the open, lance the boil as it were, she was happy to oblige.

"I won't deny that when I was that girl, I hoped my love could…change things. That you would at least consider staying. After…"

He stared at her. "But…I did."

She drew back. "You did not."

"I did," he protested. "Why do you think we didn't leave when we'd originally planned? I didn't go until the day you practically ordered me to."

The memories slammed into her. The last-second change of plans, that he'd chalked up to getting all the guys coordinated. Especially Boots, whose last local gig had been extended, and that he'd had to complete because he needed the guaranteed money. It had been a blissful time for her, when she'd let herself think he might stay after all.

But it had all ended the night she'd come to the tree house and heard him playing something new. She had waited, below, leaning against the big oak, just soaking in the amazing beauty that was Jamie Templeton's fingers on a guitar, creating something that had never existed before. And then he began to sing, low, light, bits of lyric that made her throat tighten but her heart soar.

Her entire plan—to seduce him into some more mad, wild sex—had changed in that moment. She remembered untying the T-shirt she'd knotted tight around her ribs, baring her midriff above her jeans. She remembered considering slipping over to the river to wash the makeup off, makeup she'd put on because she thought it made her more alluring.

But that was no longer what it was about. And when she went up the ladder to that place that had become their hideaway, instead of doing what her body still wanted her to do, grab him and hold on, she sat and quietly said, "Jamie Templeton, you need to get out of Dodge. The world needs to hear your music."

"Come with me," he'd said, urgently.

"You know I can't. At least, not yet. I can't leave my brother, not after he gave up his whole life to take care of me."

And she had felt seven kinds of a traitor because deep down some part of her had still hoped he would say he would stay, because he couldn't leave her. But the moment the band's first song took off she knew she had done the right thing. She just wished it hadn't come at such cost to her heart.

She stared at him now. Swallowed. This was a revelation she hadn't expected. "Are you saying you delayed because of…me?"

He nodded. "Boots was going to fly out and meet us, after he'd finished up. But by then I wasn't sure I…wanted to leave at all. Because of you. I wanted time to think."

She said carefully. "It would have been nice to know that was why you delayed."

"Why else would I change the plans? I...guess I assumed you knew."

"Like you assumed I knew you'd never been with anyone before?"

His mouth twisted. "Big mistake, huh?"

She wasn't certain how this made her feel. Soothed, of course, but it was like balm on a wound long scarred over; she wasn't sure it changed anything. And it certainly didn't change the here and now. And here and now, sitting in her car, it seemed they were going to have it out. All of it.

She reached out and shut the car's motor off. Silence settled in. He was looking at her, and she knew from his eyes—those damned, enchanting green eyes—that he understood what that gesture meant.

She took another moment, until she could say evenly, "That's ancient history." She gestured toward the house. "Right now it's about respect. First, for Aunt Millie. Leaving the home she loved, enough to pass it to you, to fall apart isn't respect. Not to mention not caring enough to even come home to sort through her things."

"Because I couldn't take it!"

It burst from him with such force it took her aback. He yanked open the car door and got out. She thought he might take off running. But he stood there staring at the post oak, and the tree house. She slowly got out on her side. Stood there, staring across the roof of her car at him.

"Did it never occur to you that that woman saved my

life, my sanity, and gave me the biggest gift anyone ever has, save one?"

Damn, he'd done it again, made her breath slam into her throat as if the airway was dammed up as tight as Lake Travis. Because she knew, from the way he looked from the tree house to her when he said it, what that "save one" referred to.

He shoved those strands of sandy hair back off his forehead. He shifted his gaze to the house, and when he went on his voice was calmer, but still sounded driven.

"She gave me the music, pushed me toward it when I didn't believe I was good enough. She never stopped. If it wasn't for her I would have spent years in the system, foster care, and I never would have even thought about picking up a guitar. I would have spent my life walking around with all this bottled up inside because I didn't know what it was."

She stared at him. She hadn't seen this Jamie in years. Since their parents had been killed, to be exact. Since that night. Hurting, nearly broken. She had no words, and suddenly felt like she'd been disciplining a puppy she hadn't realized was doing what he was doing because he was hurt. She walked around the car to stand next to him. She could almost feel the tangle of his emotions, as if they were pouring off of him like river water.

He went on, slightly less forcefully now. "I knew if I even set foot on this property again I'd break. So I trusted you to do it all, because I knew you loved her, too."

"I did," she said softly. "And it isn't that I minded doing it, it was something I could do for her, but…"

"It was my job. You think I don't know that?"

"You didn't act like it."

He took a couple of steps toward the house, staring at it. "I had to choose, Zee. Between doing something about things she was no longer here to care about, versus living up to what she always taught me, to honor commitments."

She followed him as she said, "She also always taught you about integrity. 'You can't unsay a lie.' Isn't that what she said?"

"Yes." He glanced at her, looking puzzled now. "What's that got to do with—"

"But every song you do about home is just that. A lie."

"Whoa," he said, looking shocked, even putting his hands up slightly. "Where did that come from?"

"You sing about how you love home, how you miss this place, when in truth you don't care enough to come back to even visit, except for a funeral, or when someone you owe big time calls in a favor."

He crossed the last few feet to the front porch of the house. Sat on the top step. His right elbow came up to rest on his knee. And his head sank to rest on his hand. She waited. Had almost decided the conversation was over, because he wasn't going to talk anymore. And then, in the moment before she was about to turn away, he spoke. Quietly, slowly.

"We had…momentum. We were playing dates every night. I didn't want to interrupt it. The trajectory was up, and I thought if I interrupted it, we'd fall."

"Even for just a couple of days at home?" she asked, realizing she knew little about it even as she found it hard to understand.

"It only took an instant for that car to rip our lives apart." He was whispering now. "I was afraid it would all vanish. Just like they did."

Zee nearly gasped aloud. Of all the things she'd thought he might be thinking, somehow this one had never occurred to her. That he'd been driven to grab what he could when he could, because he believed—with reason—it could one day all be taken away in a flash.

She should have known. Should have realized. If she hadn't been so wrapped up in all that damned teenaged girl angst, she would have.

She dropped down beside him. And in that moment he was nothing more than the boy who had gone through hell with her, the only one who truly understood. She slipped an arm around him, leaned against him. After a long, not quite tense moment, he matched her gesture, and with his arm around her, leaned in. She gently pressed his head down to her shoulder.

She said nothing, for this was a moment beyond words.

Chapter Fourteen

"GETTING AN EARLY start?" True said without preamble when he answered the phone.

"I figured you'd be up," Jamie said. True always got an early start.

"I am." He heard a lazy satisfaction creep into his friend's voice. "Of course, there's up, and then there's up."

And then Jamie heard a rustling of cloth and a low murmur. Hope. And it suddenly hit him what True had meant.

"Er...sorry. Didn't mean to interrupt."

"You didn't. Yet. So what's up this Sunday morning?"

Damn. "Sorry," he said again. "I've kind of lost track of what day it is." And here he thought he'd been doing good to have discovered the cell signal was stronger up in the tree house.

"Understandable."

Right. "I just wondered what the closest place would be to rent a car."

"Probably Johnson City. The used car place there'll rent

one. Why?"

The answer to that seemed pretty obvious, so Jamie was puzzled. "Because I need one?"

"Why don't you just drive the Mustang?"

Jamie blinked. Slowly turned his head to look at the garage that sat a few yards away. He supposed it was a measure of how out of it he'd been that he'd completely forgotten Aunt Millie's bright red pride and joy.

"I...didn't think of that. It's still here?"

"In the garage. Should be in good shape. Zee prepped it for long-term storage when...she realized it was going to be a while."

He swallowed. "Zee did?"

"Yeah. You know she loved riding in that car as a kid. You'll have to ask her what all she did so you can undo it. And she's got the keys. We didn't want to leave them there."

Jamie didn't know what to say. Couldn't have found the words anyway, for he'd been suddenly swamped with a memory of riding with Zee in the racy convertible with the top down, hair blowing, singing along to the country rock music Aunt Millie had loved to blast. It had been one of the few joys in that grim time, and he knew they both had treasured those moments.

He realized some time had slipped by when True said cautiously, "I thought you two had...reached a truce."

He thought of those moments yesterday when they'd held each other. It had been the first time the ache inside had eased a little.

"Yeah. Yeah, I think we did. Don't know how long it'll last, though."

"I'll have her stop by. She'll be glad to do it, glad to see it out of storage and running again."

Jamie wasn't sure the truce extended into gladness about anything, but maybe.

"Thanks. I'll let you get back to...what you were doing."

"Oh, I intend to."

Jamie was smiling when he ended the call. Damn, the man was happy. And nobody deserved it more.

He walked toward the garage, which sat a few yards to the side of the house. He hadn't even been out there yet, hadn't even thought about it. He'd done some basic cleanup, but hadn't quite been able to find the energy to tackle anything major yet, and had told True he'd let him know when he was ready.

If you ever are.

He crazily felt the urge to go running back to L.A. Back to where he could blend in among the millions, and go unnoticed by most of them. Here, in the car that had once been a familiar sight to all of Whiskey River, he might as well be in a parade with his name hung on the side.

Coward.

The self-directed chiding got him over to the building. It had carriage doors, and they were secured with a hasp and padlock that looked fairly new. True, he supposed. Or Zee.

The woman was nothing if not thorough.

So, he'd have to wait until she got here. And he could hardly expect her to drop everything and come running just because he'd decided he needed wheels. The old Zee would have, as he would have for her, but he'd given up the right to expect that the day he'd left her behind.

I wish you had come with me.

He shook his head sharply. Did he, really? There had been times, in the early going, the days of playing street fairs and backstreet bars, when they'd crashed in the van, when the only meal they'd had all day was that provided by the venue. When there had been bar fights and catcalls from people who wanted the headliner, not some no-name opening act. But they'd kept on, playing anywhere they were asked, using every online outlet they could think of, with Boots, somewhat surprisingly, becoming a master of social media.

And then "River Song" had happened. The video they'd done on less than a shoestring had gone viral. The next show had been packed with internet fans wanting to see them live. And then an actor they'd never even met had reposted the video with some praise to his four and a half million followers. The explosion still boggled him. It had landed them that opening spot at one of the biggest venues in L.A. and that was the final launch; Scorpions On Top had arrived.

That part, he would have liked her to be there for. The euphoria, the joy, the feeling of flying into the stratosphere.

With no chemical assistance.

His mouth twisted wryly. It had been around, and at that point the thing that had kept them all from indulging before—that they couldn't afford it—wasn't an issue; it was offered to them literally on a plate. He knew the guys took advantage, and even he had tried a couple of times. But as zinging as the high was, he didn't like the aftermath much. Hated more the lost time. That hurt more than what he'd be trying to avoid thinking about.

And there was always Zee, lingering in his mind. And the thought of how she'd feel if he truly dove into that life.

You got through the worst of life without falling into that pit, Jamie. Don't do it just because it's there. Please.

Her words, spoken as only a passionate—God, how passionate—nineteen-year-old can, echoed in his head as he walked back to the house. He went inside, from room to room, making a mental list of what he'd need to get it fit to live in. Cleaning stuff mostly. The inside wasn't in bad shape; it had just accumulated a lot of dust, cobwebs, and such. He smiled, remembering True's tale about Hope and the dust mop. He'd found the thing in the old pantry, along with some other cleaning implements that looked usable, so he was good there. Lots of things to be tightened up here, broken free there. He'd have to check what tools were in the garage; Aunt Millie had been fairly handy, always willing to try something herself before she called for help. He added a possible stop at the hardware store to his list, for rust remover if nothing else. Eventually he'd need paint, but that was down the road.

He went back outside. Started dragging more stuff to the big pile he was building near the driveway. Bits of wood and trash that had collected against the side of the house when the wind kicked up. If it was winter he'd just start a burn pile, but it was already pushing eighty degrees most days and he didn't want to risk it. There had been a time when he might have thought burning the place down was the answer to the pain, but he was past that now. He hoped.

He had just dropped a big branch that looked like it was from a pecan tree—which was odd, since there wasn't one anywhere on the property—on the pile when he heard the car. Looked up, toward the main road, and spotted a flash of green through the hedge that ran alongside.

...driving a car almost the exact color of your eyes.

Kelsey's words came back to him in a rush. Surely that wasn't the real reason Zee's car was green. It was probably the only thing they had that wasn't black, a rough go in a Texas summer, or silver, which she had once joked was a cop-out for those who couldn't decide on a real color.

One of the boards on the pile started to slip, threatening to bring it all sliding down. He grabbed at it, and ended up with a rather vicious splinter jammed into his thumb. He was glad of the distraction despite the fact that it hurt like a son of a gun. He kept his eyes on it as he tugged at it, but tracked her approach by the sound of the tires as she turned onto the gravel drive. The sound ceased as she slowed to a halt a few feet away.

When he heard her footsteps, he couldn't maintain what was more pretense than anything, and he looked up.

Damn.

No one, but no one, filled out a pair of jeans like tall, long-legged Zee Mahan. And that silky T-shirt she wore flowed over curves he'd once known so well, although they were just a bit more…womanly now, minus the coltish lankiness of the years when she'd started the final growth spurt that put her at a gorgeous five foot eight.

He found himself fixated on the belt on those jeans, and the way it moved from level as she walked. Those hips…

A blast of heat shot through him, wiping all awareness of the pain in his hand out of his head. How well he remembered his hands there, pulling her close, tight, as he slid into her welcoming, slick heat.

Double damn.

"What's wrong?"

His gaze shot to her face. She was frowning.

"Splinter," he managed to get out, while inwardly tamping down unruly thoughts.

She glanced at the pile of debris. The frown deepened. "Shouldn't you be watching out for your hands? You can't play if you rip them up."

Doesn't matter anymore.

He almost said it aloud, managing at the last moment to

change it to, "It'll heal."

She was still frowning. "You know, you could hire somebody to do this."

That gave him back his control. "Will you make up your mind? I thought you wanted me to do this."

She blinked. Then gave him a rather rueful smile. "I guess that was contrary of me, wasn't it? Sorry. I was just worried about your hands."

That brought him back to an awareness of the pain in his thumb, and he lifted his hand again to look at the jagged bit of wood. Tried for it again, unsuccessfully. "Can't get a grip," he said, then groaned inwardly at the accuracy of those words in so many ways.

"Want me to try?" He looked at her. "Fingernails," she explained with a wave of her hand, indeed tipped with more fingernail—and just now with a rose-colored polish—than he had, although she'd never gone in for the more flashy manicures that were so common in L.A.

"Please," he said. And again he thought of all the ways that plea could be meant.

Good thing that for all her skills, she's not a mind-reader. Even if it does seem that way sometimes.

She took his hand, rested it against her left palm.

Damn. You didn't think this through.

She reached for the splinter with the fingers of her right hand. Those long, supple fingers that had wrung gasps out of him as she touched him everywhere she could reach.

Stop it!

"Just do it."

She glanced at his face. Frowned again. "It's that bad?"

He realized he'd clenched his jaw, and that she thought it was in pain. Which, in a way, it was. He consciously released it. "No. I'm just a wuss."

She raised one delicately arched brow at him before she looked back at his thumb. "This from the guy who ran half a mile on a broken foot to get help for me when we crashed Aunt Millie's motorcycle?"

He went still. He hadn't thought of that in years. He let out a half-chuckle. "God, I thought she was going to be so pissed."

Time I got rid of that thing anyway. I prefer four wheels under me these days.

You're not going to yell at us?

Is that what I should do? But here I am, more worried about you than a thing.

We're sorry. Really.

I'll settle for scared out of ever doing something silly like that again. There's an art to riding a bike, you know.

Yeah, we learned that.

I'm glad you wore the helmets. That wicked smile. *Even though riding with the wind in your hair feels so much better.*

"She was wonderful," Zee whispered, as if she'd just run through the same exchange in her head.

"Yes," Jamie said. And then jerked slightly as she yanked the splinter out of his thumb without warning.

"There," she said, inspecting the sliver of wood. "That's

got some rough edges though. Could be bits left."

"They'll fester out."

It was bleeding now, red running in a tiny stream down toward his palm.

"I don't guess you have any first aid stuff here?"

He pressed his fingers against the small wound. "It'll stop."

"I was more worried about clean."

"It'll be fine, Zee. Thank you."

She met his gaze then. Sighed audibly. "I know, I'm fussing."

"Yes. Why?"

"Because I'm afraid our…truce won't last."

He was afraid of the same thing. But he guessed it was for different reasons. He was afraid he'd blow it, because he didn't know if he could be just friends. Not with Zee Mahan, the only woman who had ever owned his heart.

Chapter Fifteen

JAMIE TOOK THE keys Zee handed him.
"We made the decision it would be just as safe here as in a rented storage," she said. He nodded. "You were already paying for storing all the contents of the house, so—"

"It's fine. I would have done the same." His mouth tightened. "I should have."

"Yeah, well." She wouldn't argue with that. "Would you rather be alone?"

He glanced at her. Had she said that just a bit too carefully? "True said you took care of it."

She shrugged. Why not, it worked for him, didn't it?

"Then you should be here."

They started toward the garage. "I wonder what kind of shape she's in?"

Why do you call it a she, Aunt Millie?

Tradition. Sailing ships, sleek cars...call me old-school, but why would I want to lose a tradition that likens what is thought most beautiful to a female? It's quite a compliment.

Yes, but...couldn't it be a he?

Zinnia my love, that's your decision. You can make of your life and the things in it anything you want.

"Zee?"

She snapped back to the present. "Sorry. Lost in a memory there." She met his gaze, held it. "I still miss her."

"So do I," he said softly. She didn't think her expression changed, but he added, "I know you don't think so, but—"

"I never thought you didn't love her or grieve her passing." Deck's words flashed through her mind again. "Something else Deck said was that someone needing to be alone until they can at least see the other side doesn't mean they care any less, hurt any less, they just handle it differently."

"He's full of hard-won wisdom."

"He also said," she added, with self-directed tartness, "that there are a lot of people who think that way is wrong and theirs right."

For a moment his gaze sharpened, but then he looked away without saying a word. Which was answer enough.

I knew if I even set foot on this property again I'd break. So I trusted you to do it all, because I knew you loved her, too.

She steeled herself to it because she had to. She owed it to him. "I'm sorry, Jamie. I was one of those, who didn't understand there was more than one way. I thought because you…needed us when our parents died, that it would be the same."

His gaze snapped back. "I was a kid then."

"Is that it? We both grew up. But I hung on to what I

still had and you...started letting go?"

She hadn't meant that to apply to them, to him letting her go, but he was looking at her as if she'd said it.

"Does everything always have to be neck-deep?" he finally said, sounding as weary as he'd looked when he'd gotten off the plane.

So. Back to the shallows. Men...

She managed not to sniff. "You going to open the garage?"

Accepting the change of subject, he looked at the keys she'd given him. She saw him catch the key fob, shaped like the car they were about to unveil. Millie used to joke about that, saying she wanted to be able to find the car keys at a touch, because if the whole place ever caught fire, the rest could burn but she'd by gosh save that car.

"It was his, you know. The car."

"His?" It took her a second. "You mean...the man in the photos? The soldier?"

He nodded. "I found the original paperwork in the glove box last time I drove it. She kept it." He was still touching the tiny car on the ring. And his voice was tight when he said, "When I asked her she said that car was as close as she could get to being in his arms."

"No wonder she loved it so much. I wish we'd known back then, when we used to ride in it as kids."

"We wouldn't have understood, really. Even later I couldn't understand how she could bear even having it around, let alone driving it like she did."

She was suddenly swamped with memories. And realized the difference had been there all along; where she had clung to and taken comfort from her parents' things, Jamie had wanted them out of sight.

But their things, they make them feel close again.
No, Zee. All they do is remind me they're gone.

And then another memory, this time of her brother, who had wanted Hope to do what he would do in her situation, face down the threat and take her life back. And she herself telling him that what was right for him might not be right for Hope, and that he couldn't decide that for her.

But hadn't she done just that with Jamie? She grieved in her way, and had expected him to do the same. And when he didn't, she had assumed it meant he wasn't grieving at all, or at least not as much as he should for the woman who'd changed her entire life for him. That he hadn't come home to see to her things because they didn't matter to him.

Because I couldn't take it!

Maybe Deck had been right. "Avoiding it gives the scar time to form," she said softly, gently now, "but it doesn't change it."

"No, it doesn't," he agreed, sounding weary again. "Nothing ever, ever changes it."

Chapter Sixteen

JAMIE STARED AT the covered shape. Masked yet so familiar. His gaze skittered around the garage. Past the workbench with its tool drawers, which he'd check before he went to the hardware store. His gaze snagged on the potting bench where Aunt Millie's gardening tools still were, although the big-brimmed hat she usually wore when working out in the hot sun was not on its usual hook. Probably just as well; critters seemed able to get into even the best-sealed working garage. But it dug at that deep, hidden tear inside him, this further sign that she was gone.

It took him a moment to steel himself, to get his mind into logistics mode. He couldn't think about the emotions attached to this, it was simply a car that had been stored for a long time and would need attention to get rolling again. He walked toward the car. Wondered with a frown why he was suddenly thinking of toothpaste. Shook it off.

He selected the smallest of the three keys on the ring, the one that went to the tiny padlock on the cable that held the car cover in place. He bent to unlock it, and without a word

Zee walked to the other side and bent to tug the cable now attached only on that side clear. She coiled the plastic-protected metal cable carefully, so that it wouldn't accidentally ding the car. He walked to the back of the car to tug the heavy chamois-like cover free; Millie had taught him early that, in her view, it was easier to put it on front to back, so you had to take it off and roll it up back to front. The sixteen-year-old he'd been, beyond excited at learning to drive in the classic Mustang, would likely have just yanked it off and left it in a pile to be straightened out later.

He noticed a large object, also covered, in the back corner of the garage. Once he had the back of the cover pulled clear—with Zee helping on the other side, to keep it tidy—he realized what the object was. Or rather what they were. Because the Mustang was up on jacks.

"The tires."

"Yes. I pulled them off so there wouldn't be flat spots." Once she realized he wasn't coming back, Jamie thought. But she wasn't sniping, she was just explaining. "Things got crazy at work, and I couldn't get over to drive it often enough, and those are expensive tires."

He hadn't even known she'd bothered. But he should have. "What else?"

Zee shrugged. "Washed it, waxed it, made sure the underside was clean. Blocked a few places mice might be able to get in. Hence the mousetraps, which were thankfully empty most of the time. Peppermint oil spread around helped, I think. They don't like the smell much."

Ah. The toothpaste. That explained that.

"Changed the oil," Zee continued, "so it'd have clean in there. Filled the tank to keep moisture from building up, put stabilizer in. Probably on the edge of its effectiveness by now, but it should be okay. Put it on a trickle charger. Wouldn't have bothered, but the battery was new."

"Zee," he began, but stopped because he didn't know what to say.

"So now," she went on, ticking off a list in a very Zee-like manner, "we need to check and make sure no critters made it. Belts, hoses, wires. Check for nests. Pull out the stuff I used to block entry points. Check the wipers. Fluids. Reconnect the battery. Get the tires back on, check the pressure."

"Brakes?"

She gave him a look that so reminded him of the old Zee it was nearly a punch to the gut. "Plan on needing them?"

"It's the Mustang," he said with a grin that was nearly genuine.

She laughed. It sounded nearly genuine, too. "They should be okay, might be a little rust, but that'll go fast, once she's rolling again."

He studied her for a moment, decided to risk it. "When did you get to be an expert on storing classic cars?"

The light of laughter left her eyes. "When I needed to be."

"Zee, how many times can I say I'm sorry?"

She gave him an odd look. "That wasn't aimed at you. I was missing Aunt Millie."

"Oh." He grimaced. "Sorry. World doesn't revolve around me, right?"

She gave him a look that as much as said, "Mine did, once." That was a punch to the gut. But she didn't say anything, and he wondered how big an effort it was.

His mouth tightened, but he got words out evenly enough. "Guess we grew up, huh?"

"I'm still working on that one."

"Me, too," he said softly.

Then, briskly, Zee was back to business. "Probably should wash it once all that's done. Even covered, stuff accumulates."

"Wanna help?"

He said it before he thought, thinking of all the fun times they'd had doing it back then, usually ending up wetter than the car, a nice result in a Texas summer.

But once it had also ended up with them both soaked to the skin and in the tree house, the day teenage hormones had overrun all sense and they'd given in.

"I didn't mean—"

"I didn't think you did. I'm sure you've become too much of a gourmet to want plain old hometown offerings."

He recoiled at that. In fact, the banquet was there and available, but he hadn't partaken for a very, very long time.

Which she would know, if she ever bothered to come to a show anymore.

"And how the hell would you know?"

"Did you forget I was there when you headlined in Fort Worth the first time?"

He winced inwardly. Okay, she had a point, even if it was a bit dated. That was their first tour date back in Texas after they'd lifted off, and it seemed half the city had turned out to welcome back the home-state boys made good. And half of those seemed to be women who had their own particular kind of welcome home in mind.

And he'd been amped enough, caught up in the undeniable fact that it was actually happening, that they were happening, that he'd gone a little crazy. The show had been wild, long, and damned near perfect; it seemed nobody could put a finger wrong and he hit every note dead center and felt like he could hold it forever.

It was after the last encore that things got a little fuzzy. He wasn't sure what he'd imbibed, liquid or otherwise, only that he'd awakened before dawn with a half-naked woman—a total stranger—sprawled next to him and a raging headache hammering behind his eyes.

And it wasn't until much later that he remembered that Zee had not only been there—and come backstage before the show—he'd also made sure she knew where the party was after. And Boots said she'd shown up, but he was already well on his way. Just the thought of what she'd seen made him a little queasy; she would have walked in on everything she'd feared from the beginning. He'd swear he'd never touched the woman—he had this vague memory she'd come in attached to Scott, their drummer, which put her off-limits because the Scorpions didn't poach—but he'd certainly touched the other party favors.

No wonder she'd believed it when the first, wrong news broke about the OD.

He drew in a deep breath, and turned to face her head on.

"I won't lie to you—I never have—and say I didn't fall into the swamp for a while. I did. But I climbed out that next morning, Zee, and I never went back. Even now, when—"

He cut off his own words sharply. That was a road he was not ready to travel. That led to places he hadn't acknowledged even to himself.

She was studying him. "Never?"

"Any time I was tempted, I just thought of you, and what you probably saw that night."

"I got an eyeful, all right. She was pretty, in a big-city kind of way."

"I didn't even know her name. Does that make it better, or worse?"

Her mouth twisted rather sourly. "Yes."

"Zee—"

She shook her head. A strand of that glossy dark hair fell

over one eyebrow and she brushed it back. "Look, you moved on, I moved on. Let's not explode this truce with memories we can't do anything about."

It was a sizeable peace offering. He knew he should grab it and be grateful. And he gave it his best effort.

"Agreed. Thank you."

She nodded, and went back to checking the car.

And he stood there mutely, denying even to himself that he hated the idea that she had moved on from what they'd had, even though he knew damned well he had no right.

Chapter Seventeen

"IS IT TRUE?"

Zee looked at Martha, the drugstore clerk, across the counter. She knew, she just knew what the woman was talking about. She also knew Martha was the nexus of the Whiskey River grapevine.

"Is what true?" Zee asked, figuring it was better to find out what the woman thought she knew before she admitted to something that might tell her something she didn't know. And even that thought was too convoluted for her head this Monday morning. Hence the aspirin she'd come in for.

"That he's back."

She tried to kick her mind into gear. Jamie had said he needed time before everyone found out he was home. But they had gotten the Mustang up and running yesterday, although she'd left the washing to him—she didn't want to stir up those memories again—and if he was going to start driving around in that eye-catcher, word was going to get around fast.

"You mean Alex?" she bluffed, picking a name out of the

air as Martha put a small bag down on the counter and reached into the register. "He got back last week. I'm surprised you hadn't heard yet."

"Who?" Martha said as she held out the money.

"Alex." She reached out to pick up the bag and take her change. "Isn't that who you meant?"

"No, I—"

"Sorry, have to run," she said airily. "Have a great week!"

She made her escape, half expecting the older woman to follow her outside, since she'd been the only customer in the place at the moment. And the return of Jamie Templeton was enough to not just rattle the grapevine, but sizzle it.

She got waved down by a half a dozen people just walking from the drugstore back to her car. All wanting to know a variation on the same theme.

Is it true?

Did he OD, too? Is that why they canceled the rest of the tour?

Is he really back, or is he in rehab?

How long is he staying?

Weren't you two a thing in high school?

When is he coming into town, so I can grab a pic to post?

None of them were close friends, so she ended up giving them shrugs and "How would I know?" or "No idea," answers.

When she got home she uncharacteristically pulled her car into the garage and shut the door. She didn't want anyone casually driving by seeing it and deciding to stop and ask more of those questions. And when she went inside she left the blinds closed, hoping it would appear as if she weren't home.

Of course, that could send them out to Aunt Millie's, looking. Those who knew enough to know that's where he'd likely be. Then again, those who knew also likely knew the place wasn't really fit to live in.

She was making a pretense of working—and even got one or two things done—when it belatedly hit her that it said something that Jamie, who had likely gotten quite used to the perks of the road, and since they'd started having major success had traveled first class, would even stay in such conditions. Sleeping in the freaking tree house. That would be taking getting back to your roots a bit far.

Then again, since he'd built the thing, maybe not.

She stared toward the closed blinds, looking at the spring sunlight pouring in around the edges. Wondered if he had any idea what a storm he had stirred up by coming home.

People get weird.

Was this what he'd meant? She'd been thinking more along the lines of people swarming him wanting autographs and such. Not that they wanted every bloody detail of his life and what had brought him back here. Maybe he hadn't expected that here, in Whiskey River. Maybe he thought they'd be more…calm about it. Accepting. Maybe most even were.

But enough were not that it was nagging at her. He

should know. Because sooner or later, and probably sooner, somebody—or a lot of somebodies—would figure out where he likely was. And Aunt Millie's place didn't even have a fence.

He should stay at Declan and Kelsey's place. They could hold off a horde from that tower if they had to. And she was certain they would welcome him. He could even hide out, if that's what he needed to do. Deck had mentioned that once his agent had come to check on him, he'd put the man in the other end of the house and they had to schedule a meeting in the middle or they never would have seen each other.

She should go tell him that. He might not have thought of it. Might have thought he had to stay at Millie's.

Isn't that what you wanted me to do? Take care of Millie's place?

The contradiction jabbed at her. But she hadn't realized then. She supposed she should have, but she'd trusted Whiskey River to let him be if that's what he wanted. She hadn't accounted for those few she guessed were probably in every town, who couldn't do that. Who had to spice up their own dull lives by intruding on others. Or who wanted to catch some photo to blast all over social media, and revel in the secondhand attention, as if it somehow lifted them to the level of their subject.

And for all she knew, Jamie was counting on the same thing, being left alone because this was Whiskey River, his hometown. But who knew what might happen when word got around where he was.

Maybe he'd better make his first project building a fence, with a big old gate like Deck's.

She grabbed up her phone and called her brother. He was on a remodel consultation this morning, and she'd heard him leave early, so maybe that meant he'd finish early. But it went to voice mail, which usually meant he was in the middle of something. Hope she didn't even try, because she knew she and Kelsey were on their way to pick up the van they'd been donated for the outreach program.

Reluctantly, she called up the number she didn't want to call. And no matter how many times she told herself it didn't matter, they'd reached a truce, she could call him, she found it very hard to tap that icon and make the call.

Then, to add insult to it all, when she finally did he didn't answer. She didn't want to try and say this in a voice mail, so she disconnected. That left her two options. Let him find out on his own, the first time he ventured out, that a flock of vultures were in the area, or go back to Aunt Millie's. While there was a certain temptation to the first, the memory of how he'd looked when they'd picked him up at Devil's Rock made that choice impossible.

And so she found herself back in her car, retracing her tracks from yesterday. He wasn't at the house, so she headed for the garage. The Mustang sat there, gleaming, looking as if it had just rolled off the showroom floor yesterday instead of more than fifty years ago. But there was no sign of Jamie.

With a sigh she headed toward the back of the property, and the big post oak that was halfway between the house and the river.

She was still a few yards from the tree house when she heard it. The soft, dulcet sounds of that sweet old acoustic, Aunt Millie's gift that had started him on the trajectory that had surpassed even her hopes and dreams for him.

Her steps slowed as she listened to him play. Back where it had all begun, a boy with a tragedy in his past and a loved guitar in his gifted hands, in a tree house he'd built himself. The kind of stuff legends begin with.

And this song was something new, she thought, coming to a halt below the tree as she listened. No, not new, it was...familiar. But different.

It took her a good minute to realize he was taking their most upbeat, raucous, cheerful rocker and turning it into...a lament. A slow, lingering, achingly sad lament.

Once she'd recognized it she wondered why it had taken her so long—the tune was clearly there. But she never in a million years would have thought he could take that slamming, in-your-face song and turn it into this mournful, heart-wrenching thing.

And yet, there was something missing. It was as if he were playing it this way because he couldn't play it as it had been written. As if that kind of flash and fire were no longer there.

And then it stopped. Abruptly, and with a protesting

squeak of strings she could hear even from here, at the base of the tree. Silence for a long moment, and then a sound she recognized, the two fasteners on the guitar case snapping shut.

She steadied herself, uncertain why that altered version of one of her favorite songs had affected her so much. It was his, he'd written it, he had the right to play it any way he wanted. She wasn't such a purist that she would deny the artist that option, wasn't one of those who went to a live show wanting to hear exactly what they'd heard on a recording.

But this had unsettled her. More, she thought, than it should have.

The silence spun out, and finally she called up to him. "You want to drop the ladder down?"

It was a moment, long enough that she wondered if she'd completely surprised him, before his voice came down from the tree house. "It's up for a reason."

"Yeah, I figured when you didn't answer your phone. The privacy thing. But that's why I'm here." When he didn't speak again, she added with manufactured cheer, "And in case you've forgotten, I'm pretty good at climbing this tree."

After a moment there was a sigh, then a scraping sound, and the rope ladder unrolled to dangle before her. She scrambled up, thinking all the way how much she hated the way it swung around, and that next time—if there was one—she'd just climb the blasted tree.

He was sitting in the corner of the single, rough-hewn room where you could look out to the river. She fought down her instant, visceral reaction to being once more in the place where her life had changed forever. She mentally walled it off, tamped it down. She was done with showing that it still got to her.

She looked around. Tree house with a view, they'd always joked. The sleeping bag was rolled up in the opposite corner but not stuffed in the case, so he wasn't planning an immediate and swift escape at any moment. But quick, perhaps, she thought as she noticed his duffel was closed and zipped, with nothing personal lying about. Like True had told her Hope lived, when she'd first arrived. Just in case she had to run.

The only exception was a copy of Declan Bolt's latest Sam Smith adventure that sat on top of the battered black bag. The one that was so aptly titled *Light in the Darkness*. The one where the young hero had found help in an unexpected quarter, but had been afraid to trust it.

Was he reading it because it was the latest and Deck was his friend? Or was he reading it because the helplessness Sam felt in the beginning of the story was how he himself was feeling?

She wasn't even sure why she thought that. Given the circumstances she would expect him to be feeling sad, regretful, even devastated, but helpless?

He wasn't looking at her. Apparently didn't want to. So

she said something she hoped would be unexpected.

"It feels different, depending on what order it happens in."

He blinked. Turned his head. *Gotcha.*

"What?"

"It feels different, to get to know somebody whose work you already really like," she said with a nod at the book, "versus having somebody you already knew start producing work you really like."

"Oh."

"Speaking of which, that was a very…interesting version of 'Take That.' It took me a few moments to even recognize it."

He shrugged.

Okay, that was two one-syllable answers and a shrug. Try for three syllables, or two apiece?

"It wasn't just the down tempo. And nothing can take away from your talent, from the skill of your fingers on strings and frets. But there's a difference between when you're just…noodling, and when your heart's in it."

He went very still. No shrug. And no eye contact. But after a moment, she got a few syllables. She wished he hadn't.

"You're assuming there's a heart left to put in it."

Chapter Eighteen

JAMIE STARED OUT at the river, determined to keep his eyes pointed that direction. One glance at her face told him the words he hadn't meant to say had registered.

There was a moment of silence when he could almost feel her wrestling with whether to pursue what he'd nearly let slip. But then he'd always been tuned in to the moods of Zee Mahan. When his friends had griped about their girlfriends getting mad or upset for no reason, he'd always said, "There's a reason, even if it doesn't make sense to you." And the answer had always been, "Easy for you to say. You and Zee read each other's minds."

Read each other's minds...

He damned well hoped that was a skill she'd forgotten.

"You said you were here for a reason?" he asked, sharply.

"Just a warning," she said, her tone too carefully neutral to be accidental.

His mouth quirked sourly. "Only one?" The list of things she could warn him about was long and varied.

"For now. I was just in town."

"Congratulations." He could snipe, too.

He kept staring out at the river, watching the shine on the water ripple as it slid past. Finally, she spoke again. Calmly. And in that moment, she suddenly reminded him of Aunt Millie, who never reacted quite the way he'd expected. It had been one of the joys of living with her. He'd loved his parents, grieved them to this day, but Aunt Millie had been an adventure.

"When you said people got weird, I thought you meant in a fan sort of way."

He glanced at her then. "I did."

"I didn't realize being a fan meant wanting to know every bloody, grim, unpleasant detail of your life."

"That," he said dryly, "is just being human."

"Not what I'd call it."

"So you don't want every bloody, grim, unpleasant detail?"

"So I'm just a fan?" she countered.

He sighed. "You know you're not."

"Then you should know it's not a matter of me wanting. It's a matter of you needing to get it out."

He looked back at the river. After a moment she spoke again.

"You used to get it all out in your music. You'd play up here for hours."

"Just did that," he pointed out.

"You were playing," she agreed. "But it was pure pain.

That song is full of sass, but you could have been a cover band for all the energy that was in it."

He seized on the words, needing the distraction. "We have one. Out in L.A."

"A cover band?"

He nodded. "They call themselves Can of Worms."

She laughed, sounding as if it had been startled out of her. He risked a glance. She was smiling. "They obviously heard the story of how you got your name."

He nodded. "They're actually not bad. I went to see them once."

"They must have been in heaven."

"I just snuck in." His mouth quirked upward. "Their front man is a lot prettier than me."

"Jamie Ford Templeton, there's not a man alive prettier than you."

"And there's not a woman alive prettier than you, Zinnia Rose Mahan."

That easily they slipped back into it, the words they'd once said so often. He hadn't intended it, not really, because he hadn't expected her to say the old mantra. But now that she had, all he could seem to do was sit here and stare at her, remembering when she had said the words and meant them, when he had held and treasured her heart.

"Do you remember?" he asked softly. "When we talked about everything, solved all the world's problems with youthful ease and ignorance?"

"And now we can't even talk about our own."

"Do you have problems, Zee? Besides that idiot who finally came home, I mean?"

She looked startled. Then slowly, tentatively, she smiled. "Besides him, my life's actually pretty rosy right now. The guy who deserves more happiness than anyone in Whiskey River finally has it, so I'm good. Admittedly, Hope wasn't a Whiskey River girl, but she is now, so that'll do."

He shook his head in slow wonder as he looked at her. "You love this place down to your bones, don't you?"

"It's home," she said simply.

"You said there were other places you'd like to see. Where?"

She looked thoughtful. "Seen the southwest pretty much, so…Montana. The Dakotas."

"The wilder places," he said. "No desire to visit the big cities? New York, San Francisco?"

"Maybe to fly over." Her nose crinkled in that way that had always made him smile. "All of this is avoiding the point."

"The point of what?"

"Why I came out here. To warn you."

"Of piranhas circling?"

She grimaced. "I thought vultures, but that likeness is a little more apt."

"I'll take them over the sharks of L.A."

Her head tilted as she looked at him quizzically. "If it

was so bad, then why did you stay?"

"Because that's where it took off."

"But this is where it began."

And where it will likely end.

He suppressed a shiver. Zee's gaze sharpened. Woman never missed a thing, and she knew him too damned well. "You said you weren't using. Was that true?"

He realized where her mind had gone, that she'd thought the shiver a sign. He couldn't blame her, after what had happened to Derek, but that didn't mean her doubts didn't rankle.

"What do you want, a story for those piranhas? I'd rather you just fed me to the sharks."

For a moment she said nothing. Then she stood up. "I only came to warn you about them. I thought you might want to get it over with in town, where you can escape. Sooner or later someone will figure out you're here, and if the curiosity isn't assuaged, they'll show up here."

She turned to head for the ladder.

"Zee."

She stopped, but she didn't turn back to look at him. He couldn't get the next words out. He hadn't told anyone, not even True, how crazy it had gotten. How far from his roots he'd gotten. He swallowed tightly. Forced himself to speak.

"I thought…at first it was just being away, where nobody knew me. It was heady territory, for a kid from Whiskey River. Bright lights and big city isn't just a meme, it's the truth and it's addicting."

She was listening, although she still didn't turn around.

"That headiness, I thought it was freedom. And I won't deny I went a little crazy, wondering why I'd never realized how trapped I'd been. But that morning after Fort Worth I woke up feeling like hell, and finally realized what I'd thought was freedom was just being out of control. And where I was headed if I kept going. More important, I realized what was missing."

She did turn then. She didn't speak, but those wide blue eyes were fastened on him. She deserved this, he thought. And he hadn't realized how much until now.

"There was no one to do what you did—what you'd always done—for me. Kept me centered, anchored."

She finally spoke then. "Some would say anchored is the same as holding back."

"Only someone who hasn't been too close to hurtling out into space."

"Why didn't you come home then?"

"Because the next day we got asked to open at the Staples Center."

The show that had begun the dazzling rise, the bursting into awareness of the newest, hottest band around, never mind that they'd been slogging around the edges for nearly two years. He'd called Zee that night, a little delirious with excitement.

He realized suddenly he had a chance to ask something

he'd always wondered about. Was doing it before he thought about it.

"Did you know? That night? About Aunt Millie?"

She smiled sadly. "Yes."

So even as spitting mad as she'd been at him then Zee had gone along with his aunt's wishes, not to tell him about her illness then. She'd told him herself, later, that she hadn't wanted anything to detract from the excitement she could hear in his voice. And later, when she had told him, in her blunt, reality-accepting way, she softened it by saying she'd had the best things in life already: a soul mate, a child she adored, and now to see that child achieve a dream denied to most.

"I'm so glad she lived long enough to see you hit the big time," Zee said softly.

He lowered his gaze to the guitar case. "She had a lot of faith in me."

"She did. And rightfully so, obviously." After a moment she added, "She never stopped talking about those two weeks on the road with you."

He'd managed that, before she'd gotten too ill to travel, before the cancer had her in too much pain to even move. And the guys, especially Boots, had treated her like visiting royalty, and watching that had inspired what would become their biggest hit, "Those Who Came Before." It had inspired even more than a song, but he didn't want to say anything about that until it was all final.

"I still miss her, so damned much." His throat was almost too tight for the words to get out.

"I know." His gaze snapped back to her face. "But she was so proud and happy, Jamie. And you gave her that."

And then Zee was gone, barely making a sound as she went down the ladder.

For a moment, Jamie just sat there. Heard her car—that damned green car—start, then the sound of tires on the gravel drive.

Emotion was choking him. If he didn't do something, if he didn't move right now he was going to be crying like a baby in the next ten seconds. He scrambled to his feet. Dug in his pocket for the keys to the Mustang.

"Might as well get it over with," he muttered.

He went to the small landing at the front of the tree house, bent, grabbed the edge and dropped to the ground, foregoing the ladder.

Whiskey River, here I come.

Chapter Nineteen

THE PIRANHAS WERE pleasantly absent, at least at first. The gleaming red classic car turned a few heads, but he'd left the top up both to give what cover it could to him, and because he was going to be picking up things that he'd need to secure. Although he was halfway there when he remembered this was Whiskey River, not L.A., and the likelihood of anyone stealing cleaning supplies out of his car was just south of nil.

As it turned out he was able to ease into it; the guy at the hardware store wasn't familiar, and he had no idea who Jamie was. But he was immensely helpful; when Jamie told him what he needed to do, he walked around the store with him, making suggestions.

"Wood floors? This'll do it. For tile, here, this stuff'll cut through layers of grime. And this brush, see how it's angled? Corners and edges. But don't use it on the wood."

Jamie tossed the stuff into the cart.

"Windows?" the man with the name tag labeled Martin pinned onto his chest asked.

"Yeah, but not too many. A lot are broken and have to be replaced."

"You got a guy for that? Because I know a guy."

"So do I."

"Mine's the best in town at getting stuff done," Martin said.

Jamie found himself grinning. "Unless his name's Mahan, you're wrong."

Martin looked startled, then laughed. "Yeah, that's the guy. I was thinking you were new here, but if you know about True, maybe not."

"Not new," Jamie said, "but I've been gone for a while."

A booming voice came from behind him. "And it's damned well about time you came home, son."

He turned around to see Brant Barker, who had run the gas station and mechanic's shop just off the town square for as long as Jamie could remember. "Mr. Barker."

"I saw that sweet old buggy outside, so I had to make sure nobody'd absconded with it."

"Just me."

The tall, not quite burly man lifted his worn Rangers cap, ran a hand over a head of still-thick silver hair, then resettled the cap.

"That doesn't count. Millie always meant for you to have it."

There was a sadness in his voice that triggered a memory. "And you kept it running for her."

Brant studied him for a moment. Something decided him, and he said, "I tried for years to get that woman to marry me, you know."

Jamie blinked. "Uh...no. I didn't know."

"Well, I did. But she never quite got over losing that soldier of hers."

"I know." He wasn't sure what else to say, so he went with the truth. "I know she did like you, a lot. She always said you were a good man. The kind she'd want, if she was looking."

Brant stared at him for a moment, and then a warm but sad smile spread across his face. "Thank you for telling me that, son."

Jamie gave him an echoing smile. "Seems like something you should know."

"She was damned proud of you, boy. You and that music of yours gave her more happiness toward the end than anything else."

He said nothing about what had sent him running home, for which Jamie was grateful. In fact, he was feeling pretty good after that, and it lasted through stops at the bakery—okay, so he was a sucker for the smell of cinnamon rolls—then Riva's Java for a cup of coffee, where Riva herself offered condolences on both Derek and Millie, since she hadn't seen him since his aunt had died. There was no dig in her tone when she said that; either she saw nothing odd in him staying away, or thought it was none of her business. He was guessing the latter; she did a good job of never antagonizing a customer.

It kind of ended with his stop at the drugstore for toothpaste. He winced inwardly the moment he walked past the checkout counter. He'd forgotten about Martha. She gave a dramatic gasp when she saw him, putting a hand to her chest as if the shock had given her palpitations.

"Jamie Templeton!"

A for recognition.

But he managed a smile. Maybe it was for the best. Martha would have the news he was back spread all over town within the hour. He could get it all over with at once.

Besides, this way he didn't have to say a word; once she was off and running, the woman carried a conversation all by herself. Even when she asked a question—"You're not using those awful drugs, are you? Your folks raised you better than that."—she never waited for an answer before barreling on.

As he finally escaped the barrage, he'd decided he actually preferred Martha's flood to the condolences, because he could sense behind most of them the awkwardness people felt, given that Derek had in essence done it to himself. The ones about Aunt Millie were fewer, not surprising given how long it had been. And those who did mention it tended to do so with a touch of curiosity, no doubt wondering why the nephew she'd raised from age fourteen had left town again right after her funeral and never come back.

But this was Whiskey River, and no one was blatantly

mean or cruel. There was just that question mark in their voices. And he tolerated it better than he'd expected to, and was feeling fairly satisfied about venturing into town as he headed back to the Mustang.

It lasted until he walked past the barber shop. The door was jerked open just as he passed, and Charles Reid stepped out. Quickly, as if he'd been waiting to pounce.

Like a wolf spider.

Jamie smothered a groan. The proverbial grumpy old man at thirty-five. Hell, Charles—never Charlie, or Chuck—had been born grumpy and never changed. His earliest memory of the man was when he'd had to be about thirteen, and Jamie and some other five-year-olds were playing in the park on an after-school outing. Charles had stood there, frowning at them, although they were in fact being rather circumspect because one of the kindergarten teachers was there overseeing things.

It was the irrepressible Zee who had asked the teacher, Mrs. Stephenson, why the boy over there was mad at them.

"Because you're having fun," she'd answered with the laugh that had all the little boys half in love with her.

And she'd been utterly right, Jamie thought now. Charles just didn't like the sight of anyone having fun. He wondered what kind of childhood the guy must have had to have been like that so young.

"So," Charles said rather pompously. "It is you."

"Yes." *I suck at being anyone else. Hell, sometimes I suck at being me.*

"Finally come back for your girl? About time." He had not expected that. And couldn't think of a damned thing to say. "Wouldn't blame her if she doesn't take you back, though."

Jamie felt a knot deep in his gut. "I would be surprised if she did."

That seemed to take the man aback, giving Jamie enough time to mutter a "Gotta go," and get to the car.

He was back on the main road before he let himself think about what Reid had said. Take him back? Was that really what people thought, that he'd come to see if Zee would take him back? A stark, harsh longing for just that erupted in him. He fought it down.

Why on earth would they even begin to think she would? He hadn't come back to make that futile effort. How he felt didn't matter, he was certain of her feelings about him.

He'd come back because he hadn't known what else to do. Because he needed to face the truth. The final, unavoidable truth, the one that he knew in his mind, in his gut, but refused to let into his heart.

Facing it was going to be next to impossible.

But trying to get Zee to take him back would be the impossible.

Chapter Twenty

"SO YOU SURVIVED."

Jamie had heard the wheels on gravel and glanced out the window, seen the green car, so he was braced.

Or thought he was. When she appeared in the doorway—he'd left it open for air; some of this cleaning stuff would strip your sinuses as well as a dirty floor—he looked up and his breath stopped dead in his throat. In L.A. he'd seen hundreds, probably thousands of women in designer clothes, trendy outfits meant to turn heads. And yet again Zee Mahan beat them all hollow in a simple pair of jeans and that silky shirt that was the exact color of her eyes. Tall, graceful...willowy, Aunt Millie had always said of her.

Even when he could breathe again he didn't trust his voice so merely nodded.

"How bad was it?"

"Not so. I kind of forgot about Martha, then decided to just let her handle it."

"So all of Whiskey River knows by now you're back."

"Probably." He smiled ruefully. "Made it easier. At least

until I ran into ol' Charles."

She grimaced. "He's enough to ruin anybody's day."

"Wonder what made him that way?"

"Ever met his mother?" Zee countered.

"Point taken," Jamie said, smiling wider now.

She looked around at the array of tools and bottles and buckets he'd accumulated. "You know you've duplicated some of the stuff that's in storage."

He knew she'd done that, too, gone through Aunt Millie's things and put anything she thought of value in a storage garage. He swallowed, and with an effort said evenly enough, "I figured. But I wasn't...ready to face that yet."

To his relief she merely nodded. "Maybe later?"

"Yeah." He tried a smile. "You got the chest, though, right?"

Her smile then was soft, loving, but he knew it wasn't for him, it was for the woman who had left her the large cedar trunk she had treasured as a child. Zee had loved to open it just for the fresh scent, and to trace the delicate roses carved into the top.

"I cried over it for days."

He didn't know what to say to that, he who had fought that same deluge for even longer. *Avoiding it gives the scar time to form, but it doesn't change it.*

Maybe her way was smarter. Like today, just confronting Martha and getting it over with. Too bad he wasn't made that way. He didn't have the kind of emotional strength Zee had. At least, he didn't anymore, because he no longer had the outlet that had always saved him before.

Even as he dodged the painful thought he was aware he was doing it. He'd always told himself he was just postponing, until he was better able to think clearly, but deep down he was fairly certain that, just like Aunt Millie's death, postponing thinking about it forever wouldn't change a thing.

The silenced stretched out, and he grabbed at the first thing that came to mind. "I think I'll pass on the china cabinet, though."

Zee laughed. It was real, genuine, and suddenly all his tension drained away. "I can't imagine you keeping it. So not your style, with all that curlicue stuff."

In fact, he'd hated the thing from day one, and Zee knew it. "It wasn't her style, either."

"But it had been her mother's. So she kept it." He hesitated, wondering if she was hiding a jab at him in there. But there wasn't a trace of an edge in her voice, and she was still smiling. "Good thing you never met the woman, so you don't have to worry about it."

"Yeah."

"It's old, and in good shape, and I think it was expensive originally. It might be worth something, to people who go for that kind of thing. Maybe you should sell it."

"Maybe."

"There's a consignment place over in Fredericksburg,

maybe send him a picture." She gave him a sideways look, as if assessing. "Might help, if you need the money." He lifted a brow at her. She shrugged. "I just know hitting it big in the music business isn't like it was in the old days, when you signed with a record label and had it made."

"Or got ripped off."

"That, too. But it's different now."

His mouth quirked. "Yeah. Streaming, piracy, kind of took the foundation out from under. But it opened up a lot of doors."

"Like your internet channel?"

He nodded. That was one thing he'd done right; with Boots' help he'd had Scorpions established as a presence on the internet before they ever started out on the road. "And some other online outlets. Between that and touring, playing live and selling merch, we did okay. A lot better than okay, actually."

"And you just walked away from it."

"Yeah."

He wasn't, in fact, broke, far from it. He'd learned that from Aunt Millie as well, and the moment good money had started coming in, he'd started socking a big part of it away, living on a much lower scale than some of his counterparts, and content with it. And it had given him enough now to fund something close to his heart and still get by, which right now was all he wanted.

But the way she was looking at him fired something deep

inside, and he asked softly, "Worried about me, Zinnia Rose?"

She frowned, either at the name or the very idea she'd be worried about him. He wondered if he'd done that on purpose, subconsciously, so he wouldn't be able to tell which.

But then she just shrugged. "Just worried you're not eating enough."

"Maybe that's good. I'm not burning it off on stage every night."

She looked around the house. "You really think you're not burning off as much doing this?"

"You got me there," he said, looking around at the house. Already this morning he'd worked harder—or at least differently—than he had in years. When she fell silent, he studied her for a long moment before asking, "Did you...need something?"

"Just wondered how your venture into town went. And I want to give you this." She handed him a small key with a plastic tag attached. "For when you're ready. The tag will get you in the gate. It's space fifty-three."

He stared down at the key. The storage space. First the garage, then the car, now this. Zee was handing him back the keys to his old life. Keys she had held, kept safe. For him.

"Unless," she said, rather too carefully, "you changed your mind and are going back?"

Slowly he shook his head. *There's no reason. Nothing left.*

But was there anything left here for him, either? Or had both of his lives died?

"So you're really staying?" she asked, and from her tone realized he'd lapsed into one of those wandering silences. He looked up then, met those vivid blue eyes that had haunted him since the day he'd chased that dream out of Whiskey River.

"I am." He sucked in a deep breath. "Even if you don't…like me much."

She caught the hesitation on the word, and he saw a spark of temper flash in her eyes. "What, you want me to love you?"

A rueful smile curved his mouth, because his mind was yelling "Yes!"

"Don't worry," he said aloud. "I know that isn't going to happen."

"How would you know?" she said coolly. "You never asked." Then her expression changed, almost matched his own rueful one. "But then, you never had to before, did you?"

It took him a moment to get past the jagged shard of hope that had sliced into him at her first words. "No. Because I always knew."

She just looked at him, silently. And he had no more words, nothing to break the silence. It had never been awkward with Zee before, silence. In fact, some of his most treasured memories were of the times they'd been silent together, watching the river, or the clouds, or nothing. Or when they just looked at each other, with no need for words because it was all in their eyes, because it was in their hearts.

He felt a vague twitch, the kind that once would have triggered him to remember those thoughts, those words, and find the right music for them. Hope didn't even rise in him this time; he knew better by now.

"Well," Zee said, finally breaking it, "unless you want to go to the storage place now and want moral support, I'll be on my way."

"You'd...do that?"

"I wouldn't want anyone to face that alone."

And that's all it was. The kind of favor she'd do for anyone. "The house isn't ready yet," he said.

"Then I'll be off," she said.

He followed her to the door. She stopped just outside, an odd expression on her face. She was looking out to where the cars were parked, Aunt Millie's bright red convertible and her own vivid green sedan.

"Nice color combo," she muttered.

"Dr. Seuss Christmas cars," he said.

Her head snapped around. She stared at him for a moment. And then she burst out laughing. "Exactly."

He smiled wider than he had in months. "God, I've missed your laugh." Before she could say something that would ruin the moment he put up a hand. "I know, my own fault. I could have come back sooner."

"At least to visit," she agreed. Then, after another glance at the colorful cars, she looked back at him. "But I could have visited you, too."

"After what you saw in Fort Worth? I didn't expect you to."

"About that. Boots told me you never actually…had sex with her."

He blinked. "He…did?"

"Was he lying? Covering your cute little ass?"

"No. I may have been out of it, but not that far gone. She was Scott's hookup."

"No poaching, huh?"

"Never. Not my type anyway." He took a deep breath, and met her gaze head on. "I got…lonely sometimes. But it never worked." *Because it wasn't you.*

"The lonely rock star?"

"Pretty cliché, huh," he said wryly. "But it's true."

"Why things become cliché, I guess."

He knew it was the last thing he should say but it came out anyway. "Do you really think my ass is cute?"

She gave him an incredulous look, then rolled her eyes in that very Zee way. "Me and a few million others. Male and female."

"But yours is the opinion that counts."

She gave him a different sort of look, one he couldn't interpret. She twirled her key ring in her hand. "Cute enough to kiss. Or kick," she said.

And then she was gone, headed for the car, leaving him still searching for a comeback as she drove away.

Chapter Twenty-One

"THAT BOY PAID more attention than I thought," True said between sips of coffee.

"To what?" Zee said, filling Hope's cup. She didn't have to ask what boy he was talking about, since there was only one who was a topic of conversation these days in Whiskey River.

"Remember when he used to hang out with me on jobs sometimes? Seems he learned a bit. He's got that house in decent shape already."

"With your help," Zee pointed out.

"Just with a couple of two-man jobs. The rest he's done himself. I think he's ready to move some stuff in."

"At least a bed to sleep in," Hope said.

Zee's gaze shot to her soon to be sister-in-law's face. Her expression was bland. Too carefully bland. "Something you'd like to hint at?" she asked.

"Just wondering if Kelsey's right, if you really picked out the color of your car because it matches his eyes."

Zee opened her mouth. Shut it again. She hadn't. No

way she had picked that color, even waited an extra week for it to arrive from another dealer in Dallas, just because it was the same color of Jamie's eyes. It just...

Coincidence?

Even she saw the flimsiness of that.

"Maybe I just like green," she muttered.

"Sure," True said easily. "Especially that particular green."

"Remind me to snarl at Kelsey next time I see her," she muttered.

"She'll just smile at you like you're a stubborn horse," Hope said blithely.

"That is if Deck doesn't take your head off first for daring to snarl at her," True said, nearly as cheerfully.

"Thanks, family dearest," she muttered.

"If we didn't care, we wouldn't prod," Hope said. "Take that from an expert at being prodded by an expert."

"Do not even go there. That's my brother you're talking about...prodding you."

Hope burst out laughing. True looked smugly pleased. And Zee found herself smiling.

Later, when they had gone and she went out to her car, she stood for a moment staring at it in the Texas sun. It wasn't exactly the color of Jamie's eyes. Because his eyes had little wedges of lighter green amid the rest. Hard to get that in a car paint job.

But it was close enough, and she had to ruefully admit

there was likely some truth to Kelsey's theory. And she didn't know which made her feel sillier, that she'd done it, or that she hadn't realized—or at least admitted—it until now.

She went back inside, stopped inside the door and just stood, having trouble trying to mentally organize her day. Pretty soon she was grimacing at her own indecisiveness. Telling herself that's what happens when you don't have enough to do, you get to thinking you have all the time in the world.

Like Derek probably did?

She had never met him, but she knew he was—had been—younger than Jamie. Probably still thought he was immortal. Whereas Jamie, and she herself, had learned at age fourteen that no one, not even those who seem the strongest and most invincible were immortal. They—

She heard the distinctive thrum of the Mustang's engine and whirled around in time to see the bright red car pull into the driveway behind hers. Those Dr. Seuss colors, she thought, and couldn't help smiling. Maybe her car was Grinch green, but that meant so were his eyes. And for all his sins, that was a nickname that would never apply to Jamie Templeton.

This was the first time he'd come to her, and she found she felt a bit edgy, wondering why. She watched, from the safety of her office, as he got out of the car. He already looked better, less hollow than he had. And he moved better, too, with more of his usual grace.

See, Jamie? Only ten days back home and you're looking like your old self again.

And suddenly she was moving, heading for the door. Realized she was nearly running, like the old days when just the sight of him made her world right and she couldn't wait to greet him. She made herself slow down, but she still got to the door before he did.

"Hey," he said, looking slightly self-conscious, as if now that he was here he wasn't sure why. Or that he wanted to be.

"You look...better."

He gave her a half-smile. "From what you said, that wouldn't take much."

"You did look pretty much like hell when you got here," she said frankly.

"Felt it, too. Now I feel like I'm at least doing something."

She grimaced. "Better than I'm doing today."

"Then...would you come with me?"

She blinked, then belatedly realized he was holding up the key to the storage space. "Oh."

"I need..." he began, then hesitated.

"To know where I put everything. Of course. But are you sure you don't need True and his truck?"

"Not yet." His voice was quiet when he added, "I was going to say I need that moral support. Nobody's ever done that for me better than you." For a moment all she could do was stare at him. And then he grinned, that quick, flashing, brilliant Jamie grin. "Besides, you know you want a ride in the Mustang with the top down."

In the face of that, there was only one answer she could give. "Let's go."

IT WAS GOOD to be home, Jamie finally admitted as they waved at a grinning Trey Kelly going the other way, pulling a horse trailer with the Kelly's Champs logo.

"People seemed to be getting over the shock," Zee said.

"Yeah. The people who knew me before are almost back to normal."

"You mean treating you like the kid they remember?"

He glanced over at her. "Some. Old man Johnson yelled at me to stay off his lawn. But he was smiling."

Zee laughed. And the sound of it was brighter than the sun pouring down, warming his shoulders as the wind of their passage tossed their hair.

"I like your hair like this," he said.

"Short? It's less of a time sink."

"I meant all wispy and tousled." *And the way it leaves the nape of your neck bare. Even if it does make me want to kiss it.*

"Windblown, you mean?"

"Whatever. I just like it. It's sexy."

He'd said it without thinking about it much, but the

look she gave him was like a roundhouse to the stomach.

"It is," he said stubbornly.

"So it wasn't before?" When he'd left Whiskey River, her hair had been halfway down her back.

He looked at her as they stopped at the corner in the town square. "I didn't say that, and quit trying to pick a fight."

"I wasn't." Her mouth quirked wryly. "I just don't know how to handle it when you say things like that."

"Why? I used to say them all the time."

"Exactly. Used to. When we were…an us."

"You mean when I had the right?"

"Yes."

That was all she said, and the words just hung there between them. Because that said it all, he thought rather grimly. He drove on in silence. When the road ahead was empty, he risked a glance at her. "Sometimes what we think we want isn't really what we want."

She looked startled. Then thoughtful. "Was that aimed at me, or you?"

"Yes."

She sighed. "I got very tired of wrestling with myself."

"The war between heart and mind has been going on for a very long time," he said as he moved to the left slightly to clear a bicyclist who looked geared up for a cross-country ride.

"Who usually wins?" She sounded so glum he nearly

smiled, but somehow that didn't seem wise just now.

"I think they just trade off," he said. "If you're lucky, the right one wins when it needs to, and it comes out about even."

"I'm not sure mine's been even for a while now."

"True was worried about you. After I left."

She blinked. "What?"

"He called to ask me what the hell I'd done to you. That was the first I knew of…how angry you were."

She was quiet for a moment. Looked thoughtful. Then she asked, "Was that right around Thanksgiving?"

He flicked her a glance. "Yeah. Why?"

"First time he asked me how we'd left it."

"Oh." He took in a deep breath of his own before saying, "I gather since he didn't come hunting me down, you said you told me to go."

"I did. I've never denied that."

"But?"

"I was foolish. And young. I really thought you might come home for the holidays."

"That's one of the best tour legs."

"I know that." The slightest bit of tension had come into her voice, and he realized he was hearing a faint echo of that war she'd talked about, from all those years ago. "I just didn't realize it then. I didn't know much about the business end of it all."

Jamie smiled wryly. "Believe me, neither did I in the beginning. If Rob hadn't taken us on, we would have made a serious mess of it all. As it is, we'll all be okay until…we decide what we're going to do."

A silver coupe approached, heading into town. He didn't know who it was. He was long gone from the days where he knew what kind of car everyone he knew drove, but a light tap from the horn told him they'd recognized him.

"Another fan," she said, but there was no bite in it.

"More likely they just liked the car."

He felt her gaze, but kept his eyes on the road because they were nearing the storage facility. "You never did get a big head about it, did you?"

"Oh, I did. When we were flying high. But life's got a way of slapping you down."

"Like taking away the people you love most?"

"Yeah."

And then taking away the only reason you were able to keep going.

Chapter Twenty-Two

ZEE WATCHED AS he stood in front of the sliding metal door, staring at the padlock as if to unlock it would be to unleash Pandora's troubles upon the world. She glanced at the hand that held the key, saw that it was clenched around the ring until his knuckles were white.

"Even after all this time, it's really that hard?" she asked.

"I told you I couldn't—"

She waved a hand and shook her head. "I wasn't criticizing. Not anymore. I was genuinely asking. I only had to do a…second round of this, after our parents were killed, because True sorted it all out it first. I guess I'm only now truly realizing what it must have been like for him."

"Middle rung of hell?" Jamie suggested.

She winced. "You always did have a way with words."

For a moment he just stood there, then he asked softly, "Would she have felt the way you did? That I didn't…care enough, love her enough, to come back right away?"

"I hope I have the grace to admit when I've been as wrong as I was. It was stupid of me to think everyone grieved in the same way. And arrogant to think that way was my way. So the answer is no. Aunt Millie knew you, knew your heart. And she loved you to the depths of her soul, and would have forgiven you if you'd danced on her grave."

"God, Zee…"

She barely realized he'd moved before his arms were around her. For a split second she thought about resisting; they were not as they had once been, and there had been too much time and rough water under that particular bridge. But something in his voice, in the way he'd looked forestalled her, and instead she slipped her arms around him.

For a long moment they just stood there. They fit together as well as ever, and his arms were strong, familiar, his body still long, lean, and full of grace. He made her feel not just sheltered, but safe as well, and she could only hope she was giving him that in return, for he was the one who needed it now.

"Do you want me to open it?" she finally, almost reluctantly asked.

"No." He released her, looked down at her with a soft, almost loving smile. The smile of the Jamie she remembered. "I'm good now."

He lifted a hand to her cheek, cupped it for a moment, and for that moment it wasn't just the smile, he was everything she remembered. Everything she had loved with all the passion of her teenaged heart.

He did better than she'd expected. His first words as he

scanned the space were, "I may need to rent a truck."

"Borrow True's."

"He's working. He can't do everything."

"Tell him that, will you?"

He grinned at her, and it was almost normal. "Think he'd believe me?"

She grinned back. "No."

They started through the accumulation of a lifetime in a fairly good state. Not that there weren't quiet, aching moments, in particular when they found the box of his parents' things that Aunt Millie had saved for him.

"She said you'd want them, someday," she told him.

He'd only nodded, and they went on. And more than once she'd caught his eyes glistening with moisture, but there was some laughter, too, when they found Aunt Millie's stuffed dragon, a wildly purple beast she had laughingly adored and kept since childhood.

"That," he said, "is definitely coming home with me now."

Home. Did he mean it? Was this home to him again? She reined in the sudden leap of her heart. Even if he did mean it, hadn't she learned the hard way that what he meant wasn't always what she meant?

A few minutes later, after she'd gone to find a particular box in the back of the space, she came back to find him clutching that silly dragon to his chest, his eyes closed.

"Jamie? Are you okay?"

"She used to let me sleep with this, when she first brought me home," he said, without opening his eyes. "She said 'I know you're too old to need a protector, so just let him be a friend.'"

Her throat tight, Zee whispered, "God, I miss that woman."

"The night True called with the news she was gone, I wanted this damned dragon more than I wanted my next breath. I wanted to curl up with him and cry. Sometimes I still do."

Zee wanted to cry herself, and the only thing that stopped her was anger. Anger not at him but at herself, for not understanding. The memory hit her again, of asking her brother back when Hope didn't think she could face the mess she'd been running from, if he could accept that Hope's way of dealing wasn't the same as his. Yet she had done the same thing with Jamie, judging his way of grieving by her own and thinking his lacking. But here it was in front of her, coming off him in palpable waves, and she felt like a complete fool.

"I'm sorry, Jamie." For so many things.

He opened his eyes then, and when he looked at her she could see the pain roiling just beneath the surface. "I was here when it all got ripped away the first time. Me being home didn't save them."

Zee stared at him. "So you thought…if you stayed away…"

"I know, it's insane, but somewhere in my head I guess I thought fate wouldn't hit again if the circumstances were different."

She swallowed. Felt slammed with another sudden understanding. Struggled for the breath to speak something she'd never admitted, even to herself. "And I stayed home because I thought I could somehow guard against it. That if we were together, nothing would happen to True."

He stared at her. She could see in his eyes that he'd never realized that was part of her refusal to go with him. How could he, when she hadn't even realized it herself until he'd said what he'd said?

Then he let out a pained laugh, again closed his eyes, and slowly shook his head. "Like we have any control at all."

"But we keep trying," she said. "And as long as we're mired in this, I have something for you." She held out the letter she'd retrieved from the box in the back. "Aunt Millie gave this to me, to give to you after…enough time had passed. She trusted me to know when the right time was, because she said no one knew you better." Her mouth twisted almost painfully. "She was wrong about that, obviously, since I couldn't even understand the simple fact that you grieved differently than I, but I decided that when you were strong enough to come here for this, that would be the time."

He hesitated. She couldn't blame him, for his name in Aunt Millie's distinctive handwriting on the front of the envelope had to be painful to see. She had been his last living relative. At least she still had True. And now Hope.

Then he reached for it. His fingers brushed over her hand, seemed to hesitate for an instant on her birthstone ring. A little shiver went through her. Then he took the envelope, but didn't open it. Instead he looked at her. And something in his expression made her say, "Did you know that when he first got home, before they tracked down Aunt Millie, he asked what would happen to you, and wondered if they'd let him adopt you?"

His eyes widened. "True said that?"

"He did. And he would have tried, if you'd really been alone."

He was silent for a long moment before saying quietly, "Your brother is the most amazing guy I've ever known."

As she'd hoped he smiled. And then he looked at the purple dragon and back at her. "Aunt Millie would have taken you, too."

"I know." He drew back slightly. "True told me she offered, if he thought it was too much for him at eighteen, and having to leave college."

"Let me guess. He said it was his responsibility so he'd do it."

"That's my bro."

He smiled, nodding slowly.

She went on in a rush. "You're not really alone, Jamie. You have us. I know we're not blood family—"

"Family isn't always blood."

It struck her suddenly, as he said words that were familiar to her from her daily play list. "Connections." Fourth Scorpions song in her rotation. *Family isn't always blood/And sometimes you have to build your own.*

"I always hoped that song was...about us. You and Aunt Millie and True and me."

"Of course it is." He gave her a sideways look. "All you had to do was ask."

"That," she said with rueful clarity, "would have required getting over myself, apparently."

The smile she got then was worth the self-humbling. "Something you've always been able to do, Zee. Eventually." His mouth quirked. "And something I had to constantly relearn."

"Hard to do with millions thinking you're all that."

"I'll just send 'em to you, and you can give them the truth."

She laughed at that, and suddenly everything was fine. He tucked the letter into a pocket. "I'll read it, when I can face it," he promised. "Back home."

And this time when he said it she knew he meant it.

At least for now, Jamie Templeton was home.

Chapter Twenty-Three

IN SOME WAYS it was like he'd never left.

After the initial buzz, things seemed to have settled. There was still the occasional…flurry when he ran into a fan. He'd gotten pretty good at recognizing the sincere ones and what they'd called the bandwagon ones, the ones who only wanted to be part of the latest big thing. Then there were the musicians, real and wannabes, who wanted to talk about his playing. Those he didn't mind so much, especially if they had some knowledge.

And then there were the girls with other things on their mind. The occasional guy who needed to know personally he was straight, but mostly the girls. He tried to be gracious, not offend anyone, but sometimes they made it difficult. At meet and greets after a show there had been security to keep things moving, but when they'd just been out on their own, it had been trickier. The guys had known that when he gave the signal—ramming both hands through his hair—it was time for one of them to call his phone and give him a tactful excuse to bail. But he didn't have them anymore.

And you don't have to be polite, they're fans of something that doesn't exist anymore.

As soon as he thought it Aunt Millie's voice rang in his head, telling him that while he didn't have to be conventional, he did have to be civil. She didn't require perfect manners, but disrespect was unacceptable.

He most liked the times when he ran into people who had known him before. To them he was still that kid who grew up here. They might admire his success, but they also remembered the rather withdrawn kid he'd been, even before that night, and didn't hold it against him.

And they treated him that way, at least enough of them that he felt almost…normal again. And it felt better than he'd ever imagined it could.

So he signed a few autographs, posed for a few selfies, and while he wasn't up to smiling mindlessly he kept a frown off his face and waved for the cameras in the hands of those too shy to approach him. Since he'd once been one of those, he understood.

But just as he was walking toward the grocery store—the old fridge still worked, amazingly enough—thinking this was going to be a snap, he heard a car door slam and quick footsteps behind him. He glanced over his shoulder, wondering what local was going to either welcome him home or rag on him for staying away so long. Instead he saw a vaguely familiar female hurrying toward him. He frowned, trying to place her, and couldn't.

But he could place her style; her whole look screamed L.A. She was dressed for a night out on the city, here at ten in the morning in Whiskey River. She couldn't have been more out of place had she carried a sign saying, "I don't belong here."

He had no doubts, but a quick glance at the car she'd emerged from confirmed his guess with rental stickers out of Austin. Damn, had she flown all the way here for…him?

Rein in the ego, boy. Lots of reasons she could be here.

"Jamie! I was starting to think I'd never find you."

Then again…

He had no idea what to say. In context, in a line after a show, he had the patter down as he thanked them for coming out. And he was, so he'd been told, good at making each one feel like they'd mattered to him in those few moments. And they did, so he always tried. With a few of the genuine ones he let it go even deeper, spent some time actually talking, about real things. Because they were the ones who mattered most, the ones he tried to reach.

And then there were the…Kims. Her name came to him suddenly, both from the times she'd draped herself over him for photos taken by friends, and cooed in his ear, and from the warnings from Rob that she was well known on the L.A. concert circuit, as a rich girl with more money than she knew what to do with. And she had apparently chosen him as her next target.

Rob's words played back in his head. *You're not the sort,*

Jamie boy, but I'll warn you anyway. One hint of encouragement, and she'll have your engagement the headline on every entertainment site on the internet. All so she can ceremoniously dump you for the next one.

She was running toward him now—a not insignificant accomplishment in those stiletto-heeled boots he supposed were her idea of Texas footwear—and he had bare seconds to think.

One hint of encouragement, Rob had said.

Okay. Right. You didn't remember that name.

"Hello," he said, working hard at putting the right amount of puzzlement into his voice as she came to a breathless halt in front of him.

"I looked for you all day yesterday." She sounded as if she were trying to be teasingly pouty. It grated. "I couldn't believe I couldn't find you in this little place."

She looked around, and he had the sense the wrinkling of her nose was real. Whiskey River was like a foreign country to her. She would never understand the hold this place had on the people who loved it.

He was carefully polite when he said, "I'm sorry, I know I've seen you before, but…" He let his voice trail off.

Her eyes widened, then narrowed. As if she'd said it, he knew she was pondering if she should play it insulted. Apparently, she decided to go for the cooing.

"Oh, you poor thing, you must be so devastated after Derek. I was so worried about you, I came all this way to help."

"You want to help? Good, I'm heading out to a friend's horse rescue. She can always use help shoveling the manure."

The woman blinked. Drew back for a moment. But she clearly wasn't one to give up easily. She reached out and put an arm around his shoulder, stepping forward to stand close. Too close.

"Horses are so pretty. I'd love to see a real one."

She wasn't giving up. Odd, it probably wouldn't have bothered him in L.A.—it happened often enough—but here it seemed…wrong. He was starting to feel as if he was in over his head. He was off his stride, and with no insulation of roadies and the guys, he was drowning here.

"Hey, baby!"

The cheerful call from behind him spun him around. Zee. He felt suddenly like a guy who had realized the lit dynamite he held was stuck to his hand. He watched her walk toward him with that long, graceful stride, that sexy, tousled hair lifting slightly. She reached him and threw her arms around him. She was close, so damn close, he could feel her warmth, see the twinkle of mischief in her eyes. God, he'd missed that, missed sassy Zee. She was so—

She kissed him.

Her mouth came down on his and blasted every rational thought out of his head. Heat erupted in him, sending fiery threads along every nerve. And it suddenly changed from a teasing gesture to something more. Much more. Her lips were soft, warm, and giving. He felt the brush of her tongue over his lips and gasped. What had started as sassy Zee turned to sexy Zee so fast he couldn't catch his breath.

The other woman said something. He didn't hear what. Couldn't even think. And when Zee broke the kiss, the only thing that mattered in that instant was that she looked as startled as he felt.

But being Zee, she recovered quickly. She glanced at the woman, smiled sweetly. "Sorry to interrupt. I know how these moments are for fangirls. But I wanted to make sure he picked up the eggs for breakfast. I'm tired of just toast."

As a slap-down and a territorial claim in one, it was the best he'd ever seen. Stiletto woman sputtered. "Who are you? I've never heard or read about anybody he—"

"Bless your heart," Zee said gently. "He's mine. And he was mine before he ever picked up a guitar."

Jamie fought down the leap his heart took at those words, knowing she was just playing a part at the moment. "That I was," he agreed. "Lock, stock, and whiskey barrel."

Zee laughed. "How very Texan of you, darling."

Jamie fought down a laugh; Zee had never called anyone darling in her life with good intent. He looked back at the woman, who was now looking more like a foiled predator. As, perhaps, she was.

He looked back at the woman, who looked ready to use her not inconsiderable claws. "Still want to help with that shoveling? Or do you need to get back to L.A. in time for the Quake shows?"

The woman stilled. "What? They're not—"

"They are now. Just booked three days down the coast, Ventura to San Diego. Justin'll be disappointed if you don't show up, I'm sure."

He was able to say it with absolute sincerity, because if there was anyone who reveled in that scene, who would give her the visibility she wanted and would partake of all she was offering, it was Quake front man Justin Kramer. And Jamie was honest enough to know where he stood on that particular value scale; as big as Scorpions had gotten, Quake was a much bigger name.

"And," he added in a low voice, as if he were letting her in on a valuable secret, "I happen to know he's doing a private show tomorrow night. I'm sure with your contacts you could find out where and get in."

The woman was on her phone before she got back in her rented car, with barely a goodbye wave.

"Did you just throw her to the wolves?" Zee asked.

"More the other way around," he said. "But Justin can take care of himself. And he does like…her sort of attention."

"She's one of those, huh? One of the minions?"

He gave her a sideways look. Thought of the last time he'd asked her to go with him. *I have loved you since I was fourteen, Jamie, but I won't be one of those women, following a rock star around. I have a life here, a good one.* "Is that what you call them?"

"It has a better ring than groupie. But I guess groupie implies some things minion doesn't."

Like sex?

He sighed, half wishing she'd just come out and ask him if he'd ever slept with the woman. Because he could honestly answer no. And that was because nothing had, or ever could, match the fire this woman started in him. It had only taken that dramatic, completely scripted kiss to prove that. Even knowing it was done specifically for the benefit of that predatory woman, Zee Mahan still sent him flying. She always had.

He rammed a hand through his hair. "Damn it, Zee—" He broke it off, sure she didn't want to hear whatever would have come next. Which he didn't know, since he'd had no idea what else to say.

"Are you mad at me?" she asked.

"Yes," he said.

She looked as if she hadn't expected that answer. And her voice went rather formal. "I'm sorry for the interruption, then. I thought you looked like you wanted rescuing."

"I was grateful for it."

She went very still. "Sorry about the kiss, then."

Sorry? Sorry about the sweetest thing that had happened to him in years? "That's what I'm mad about, all right. But not that way."

"What?"

"I'm mad because you didn't mean it."

There. It was out. Zee stared at him, and he was suddenly very aware they were having this discussion in the town square, practically in the shadow of Booze Kelly's statue.

"You've picked up a nasty habit, Jamie Templeton."

"Probably a few," he said wearily. "But which one chapped you this time?"

"You make a hell of a lot of assumptions."

And then she was gone, leaving him staring after her, wondering if she could possibly mean what it seemed like she meant.

Ironically, that was one assumption he didn't dare make.

Chapter Twenty-Four

ZEE SAT LOOKING at the sunlight dancing along the surface of the river. She sat on the bench her brother had built in this spot for just this purpose, in the shade of the knockaway trees. He'd needed, he said, a place to think. And sometimes, on the worst days, he would bring her here and they would let it out, send the grief down the river, he used to say.

Only when she was older had she realized the enormity of what True had done for her, for them. Giving up his life plans, to come home and take care of his little sister, the only family he had left. And lend a guiding hand to Jamie as well, and help Aunt Millie by fixing things that needed it, so she could focus on her own newly acquired family.

Without those two people, Zee didn't know what would have become of either one of them.

I'm mad because you didn't mean it.

Jamie was a very smart guy, but sometimes he could be thick as an adobe brick. Didn't mean it? Hadn't she never stopped meaning it? Her brother had been right that day when, in this very spot, he had told her that her breakup with Nick was inevitable.

You never give anybody a real chance, Zee. Because in your heart, you've never let go of Jamie.

She stared at the water, sliding past mostly in silence, only the rush where it narrowed past the limestone outcropping audible.

Anger is still caring...

Damn her wisdom-spouting brother anyway. She hated that he'd seen it, that she had converted her love into anger because it was easier to say she was mad at him than that she still loved him after he'd gone. Or maybe it was less...what, humiliating? Embarrassing? She'd always told everyone that she was so happy for him, that he'd gone chasing a huge dream and caught it. Only with those closest to her had she ever let the rest out.

And now he was here, and by all appearances was going to stay. For a while anyway. And then what? He would leave again? Smashing her heart all over again?

Only if you give it to him again.

She was so lost in her thoughts and memories that it didn't register that she'd heard a car. The sound ended before it even got through the tangle. But the footsteps she heard. Without turning to see who it was she glanced at her phone. She'd been sitting here for over an hour, and was no closer to cutting through the snarl of her emotions. Others came here, she knew, once they'd discovered the bench True had built. And since she obviously was making no progress, she might as well surrender the peaceful spot to someone who might.

She stood up. Turned.

Jamie.

"How did you find me?"

"True. He said you might be here."

"Remind me to thank him," she said, fighting to keep a sour note out of her voice. The last person she wanted to see when she was trying to make sense of this huge knot of feelings was the guy at the heart of it all. Especially when she was trying to forget that there were likely thousands just like Ms. L.A. who would jump him instantly given the slightest encouragement. Which he thankfully hadn't given. But then he wouldn't, not with her standing right there. Jamie had too much class for that.

Just watching him walk toward her was putting her pulse in overdrive. How did he *do* that, move like that? Like he was some barely leashed wild thing?

The same way he slips that leash on stage and enthralls thousands.

He reached the bench. Only then did she realize she'd actually sunk back down on it. She studied the grain of the wood, as if all the answers were somehow hidden there, if only she could find them.

"Your brother's not mad at me," he said.

"No. He never was. He loves you, too."

Something flashed in those vivid green eyes, as if he was

wondering exactly how she'd meant that "too."

Both ways. And more importantly, present tense.

She couldn't deny it any longer. Jamie Templeton had ever owned her heart, and hard as it was to face, he apparently still did.

He was very quiet for a moment. Then he leaned forward, resting his elbows on his knees, hands clasped, staring out at the river. "Not a day went by, not one, that I didn't wish you were with me."

Something tightened inside her at the clearly heartfelt and honest declaration. "I…wanted to be. But I couldn't."

"I know. You love this place and didn't want to leave. And couldn't leave your brother. Not then."

"It wasn't just that." If he could be this honest, didn't she owe him the same? "I couldn't handle the…glare. All the focus, the fuss, being the center of the storm as it were. And being with you, in that world…that's what it meant."

His brow furrowed, but then he nodded. "You always were that rare person, who didn't want to be the center of attention."

Of course he understood. Jamie always understood. "I'd had enough of it as the local object of pity, after the accident." She gave him the best smile she could manage. "You were much better at handling that than I was."

"That's because I hid out most of the time. You kept right on with your life. I avoided mine, except for you and Aunt Millie."

"And look what came of that," she said softly. "The most wonderful, beautiful music."

His eyes went shuttered in the instant before he looked away, went back to staring at the river. As if he'd slammed a door. She almost gaped at him, so sudden and definite had it been.

"Jamie?"

It was a moment before he spoke again. "I've truly missed this place," he said. "I think I finally understand a little of what you felt, back then. Aunt Millie told me I would, when I'd been away long enough."

"She said that?"

"She did," he said, finally looking at her again, "and that we were meant to be."

Zee blinked. "What?"

He laughed, whatever had hit him so hard a moment ago gone now. Or so tightly under wraps she couldn't see it. "Exactly what I said. She only answered that was for us to figure out."

Zee laughed in turn—she couldn't help it. "Now if that isn't a typical Aunt Millie answer!"

"She was one of a kind," he said softly.

"And we were all luckier for it," she said.

"Yes. The best thing is, she felt the same way."

And there, sitting on the bench built by her brother on the river they both loved, they were as close as they'd ever been. And she vowed that no matter what else happened or didn't, this, at least, they would keep.

Chapter Twenty-Five

WE WERE MEANT to be.

The knock on the office door startled Zee out of her contemplations. She'd been working on the spreadsheets for the last quarter, which she hated anyway, so it hadn't taken much to nudge her into a reverie.

She saved what little she'd accomplished and closed the program before getting up and heading to the outside door True had installed once they'd realized they had a going concern here with Mahan Services.

She pulled open the door and for a moment just stared. "Boots?"

The man gave her a crooked smile. She'd known him almost as long as Jamie had; the bass player out of Austin had been with Jamie almost since the beginning of the music, and together they had built the success that was Scorpions On Top.

She threw her arms around him in a fierce hug. "When did you get here? Are you staying? How are you? I'm so sorry about Derek."

Boots nodded, then answered her in order, something she remembered now he'd always done, and it made her smile. "Just got in, took an early flight out of L.A., heading back tomorrow. I'm okay. It sucked, that's for sure. We knew he had a problem, but not that bad. Hit Jamie hard, because he felt like he should have known, but Derek hid it pretty well."

So Jamie felt...what, responsible? Was that what that undertone of harsh sadness she'd been sensing was? That sense of loss even beyond that of a friend?

"Have you seen him yet?"

"That's why I'm here. I wasn't sure where he was staying. And I brought some stuff for him, from his lawyer in L.A."

"Lawyer?"

"Business paperwork, mostly. I figured if anybody'd know where he was, you would."

She wasn't sure how to interpret that, so didn't even try. "He's out at Millie's place."

Boots suddenly smiled. "Shoulda known." He held up the manila envelope in his hand. "That's what some of this is about, the other Millie's Place."

"The what?"

"You know, the hospice thing."

She blinked. Boots' expression slowly changed. "He didn't tell you?"

"We've been busy...with other things. What?"

"He's setting up a hospice support foundation in her

name. Said if it hadn't been for them she would have died in the hospital in Austin instead of here at home, and she would have hated that."

"Jamie's...doing that?"

"I figured he would have told you, since you and his aunt were so close."

"I guess we haven't gotten to that yet." Her mouth quirked. "It's been a little tense until yesterday."

"Oh." Boots looked as if he truly did not want to know about that. She didn't blame him. "Anyway, he's put a big chunk of money into it. The guys think he's crazy, but then they live higher than we do," Boots finished with a grin.

Her brow furrowed. "Just how much did he put into it?"

"A lot, that's all I know. He's going to be living lean for a bit, but he was determined." He hastened to add, "He'll be okay. He was always smart about the money, once it started coming in. This was just a big chunk all at once."

She reminded him how to get to Millie's, and after he'd gone she stood there thinking for a long, silent moment.

He'd felt responsible for Derek.

He was funding the people who had helped Aunt Millie.

Maybe Jamie Templeton hadn't changed all that much after all.

HE COULD DO this.

For the first time since he'd arrived, Jamie felt as if he could really do this. He could build—or rebuild—his life here and be…if not happy, at least content. He was sure the gnawing would start, the pull, but he'd get past that.

He had to. He would. He just didn't know how long it would take. How many times did it take for the moth to learn to avoid the flame?

Enough to fry him until he can no longer fly.

He had to admit, Boots showing up like that had been a blow. Not that he wasn't happy to see his old friend, but Boots was inextricably tied up with the band and the music and it stabbed at him. If he'd stayed much longer the question would have been asked, and that would have sliced him to ribbons.

But he'd had a plane to catch and, to Jamie's surprise, he said he had someone to get back to.

"Lynn," he had said, watching Jamie warily.

Jamie placed the woman quickly as one of the fans who had avoided the craziness, had come for the music, more importantly understood the music. She was attractive, but quietly, and didn't work on seeming anything other than what she was.

"Think I'm crazy?"

"Hell, no. She's a great lady. One of the ones who really got it."

"Yeah. Took me a while to convince her. She thinks she's too old for me."

Jamie laughed. "Good, maybe she'll keep you in line."

Relieved then, Boots had smiled. "She sends her best, by the way."

"Back at her," Jamie said, and when Boots had gone a few minutes later Jamie had been left with a much easier feeling about his old friend. It had gotten him through a good hour of work without that nagging tightness inside.

Now he looked at the area on the roof True had patched. He'd said it hadn't been bad enough to rot anything underneath, and it looked thoroughly dry now. The only thing left up here was to replace the flashing around the chimney. He'd just about have time to do that this afternoon before it got dark. He'd already picked up the supplies from the list True had given him. He got to his feet, made sure of his balance on the slope of the roof, and turned to head back to the ladder.

The ladder was gone.

He blinked. Walked to the edge. Stood there for a moment. Looked around. Then spotted the answer, a slice of green fender on the other side of the house. He must have been too intent to notice her approach.

Or you had your head too deep in a hole. Again.

But he grinned; it was so like the Zee of old, the mischievous girl who had always done things like this.

He sat down, got a grip on the edge of the roof, and swung over. From there it was a drop of only a couple of feet or so. He found her grinning back at him when he landed and turned.

"Up to your old tricks, I see."

"Just wanted to see if you were still up to it. And," she added, "I brought lunch."

"In that case, all is forgiven."

For a moment something flickered under the cheerful demeanor, and he wondered if it was one of the demons he hoped they'd vanquished yesterday. But it was gone too quickly to even put a name to.

Besides, she cared enough to bring him lunch, and that made him smile. She'd always cared.

Would she still, if she knew?

He knew the answer to that, because even before he'd discovered his life's passion, she'd cared. But she also loved the music that was so much a part of him. So maybe she'd care, but it would be…different.

"Where to?" he asked, looking at the big bag she held, from the diner in town. "The kitchen's not ready yet." He thought he could smell melted cheese and onions, and his stomach was already growling. She knew him, did this girl with the sassy hair and the big blue eyes.

"The tree house?" she suggested, startling him. But she clearly meant it. She really had let it go. And she probably meant this to prove it to him.

Moments later they were in the little space where they had spent so many hours as two lost children in an upended world, and then years later so many nights as voracious young lovers who felt as if they'd reached a place that had been inevitable.

He was on his third sizeable bite of the patty melt she'd brought when she said, "When were you going to tell me?"

He froze. His stomach knotted, threatened to send the food on a quick reverse course. How did she know? Sure, this was Zee, who'd once known him better than anyone on earth, but he'd learned a lot in the last seven years about hiding. Nobody had suspected, not even Boots. Or had he? Had he seen past the façade, and now told her? Was his arrival and her question too much to be coincidental?

He wanted to run but he couldn't move. He couldn't even think. Then the urge to curl up in a ball and hide from those eyes of hers almost overwhelmed him. He nearly shivered under the pressure.

"It's a beautiful, wonderful thing to do in her name," she said softly. "Why would you want to hide it?"

That shocked his brain back to life, but he still could only stare at her as he tried to understand.

"She would be so proud, Jamie, that you're helping the people who helped her."

Millie's Place. God, she was talking about Millie's Place. Boots must have told her.

"Oh." Well, that sounded stupid enough.

"Why didn't you say something?"

"I was…distracted."

"Oh?"

Funny how her single syllable sounded so much more mindful than his had. "And it isn't final yet, until those papers are done."

"It's still a wonderful thing. Proof that you really are still you."

That snapped him out of it. "Who else did you think I would be?"

"The careless, high-living guy I was afraid you'd turn into. I wasn't," she added in a rueful tone, "thinking at all at the time." That was so much the old Zee he smiled. It might take a while, but when she got over it, she got over it. "I'm thinking now, though," she added softly.

"Thinking what?"

"That I might like the distracted part."

He wasn't sure what made him do it, but there had always been truth between them and so he did.

"I've been distracted since you laid that lip-lock on me right there on Main Street."

"I'm sure that had nothing to do with it," she said, but she was smiling. In fact, she was looking at him...like she used to.

"How can you be sure?" It came out a little scratchy, because his throat had tightened up again.

"Good point," she said. "It might bear further testing."

He sucked in a deep breath. Hoped desperately that he would need it. "That is up to you."

"I am curious."

I'm not. Because I already know.

Her mouth merely brushed his at first. Then her soft, sweet lips took his tentatively. Just as the fire lit in him, the fire only she could ever set off, she made a tiny sound and leaned in.

He needed every bit of that breath.

Chapter Twenty-Six

SHE HADN'T EXPECTED it to be the same as when they'd begun, all those years ago. How could it be, after all this time?

And she had convinced herself the jolt she'd gotten out there on Main Street had been…something else. Told herself it was only that she hadn't kissed a man in a while.

But this wasn't even the same as that kiss out in public.

It was much, much more.

They had been kids, before. Experimenting, learning, having chosen the only person either of them could envision as a partner in this new, heated exploration. And teenage love with hormones running high had been hot, fast, and beyond memorable.

But they were adults now, so what was the explanation for the instant inferno they seemed to kindle together?

…we were meant to be.

Aunt Millie's words, spoken in that voice of his, beautiful even when he wasn't singing, echoed in her head. Like the refrain of a Scorpions song, it repeated. *Meant to be, meant to be, meant to be...*

And then she couldn't hear anything, not even her own thoughts as his tongue swept over her lips and she parted them for him. All she knew was how right it felt. This was Jamie, her Jamie, and here in this place, where they had discovered what pleasure could be had, they were together again.

It was as if they had never been apart, and yet it was different. Powerful in a different sort of way. She had the odd thought it was at least in part because this wasn't inevitable, as it had seemed back then. This was by conscious, adult choice, and that somehow made a difference.

She couldn't get enough of the taste of him, the feel of him. And only now did she realize they were on the floor of the tree house, bodies pressed together as if no time at all had passed, as if they were still those teenagers so wild they couldn't wait. In that moment that's what she felt like, that if she didn't have him, all of him, in the next minute she would die. Her body was already primed, ready, and she could feel he was, too.

He broke the kiss. Pulled back. She smothered a moan of protest. She knew it wasn't because he hadn't been into it because she could hear the harshness of his rapid breathing echoing her own, could feel the rigidness of his erection pressed against her.

"Zee," he whispered.

"You stopped," she pointed out unnecessarily.

"I...had to."

"Why?" She sounded plaintive even to her own ears.

He shifted his hands, which had slid down to her waist at some point, to his favorite spot just above the swell of her hips. He let them linger for a moment, then reluctantly pulled away. Then he cupped her face, turned her so that she was looking straight at him.

"Because I have to know if you want to go where we're headed if we don't stop."

She was slow to react, so lost was she in those green eyes. Why had she never realized that was exactly why she'd bought her car?

"Don't you?" she asked, feeling a bit sluggish.

"More than I have words for," he said, sounding fervent.

Her brows furrowed as she tried to bank the heat he'd roused in her and think. "Then what?"

"I've only been back two weeks. I'm not that guy you were afraid I'd become, but...what if I really have changed?"

His words seemed to have something more behind their surface, but she couldn't put a name to it. "Your heart hasn't changed. I know that now."

"I want this. I want you, us. God, I want it. But even more than that, I don't want us to be...like we were. Like we've been since I left. I don't want you mad at me again, Zee."

"I meant what I said. I wasn't being fair and I'm sorry."

"I know. And I know you mean it. It's who you are.

But…"

She was sitting upright now, studying him. "What is it? Are you mad at me, now? Not that I could blame you, I was kind of a—"

"You were you. You'd never have gotten mad at all if you hadn't cared."

"Loved."

He blinked.

"That's the word we're avoiding. I loved you. You loved me."

"Yes." His voice had gone low, rough. And she had the sudden wild thought that it might be because of the tense she'd used. Past. As in not now.

And she wasn't altogether certain it applied. Which rattled her enough to say the obvious, so she wouldn't say the words that had leapt to her lips. "Aren't you…haven't you wondered if…"

She saw him draw in a deep breath. And he seemed steadier when he spoke again. "It's still the same? Of course I have. Is that what this is for you? Curiosity?"

"In part," she admitted honestly. "But it's never been that simple with us."

"No. It hasn't." He tilted his head and gave her a lopsided smile. "Besides, I think we just proved it's not the same."

"We did?"

"Darlin'," he drawled, "that kiss wasn't our old fuel on the fire. It was pure dynamite."

A slow smile curved her mouth. "Yes. Yes, it was."

"But it's...impossible right now, anyway."

"Impossible?"

His mouth quirked wryly. "Unless you've got a box of condoms in your pocket."

"Oh." She glanced toward the house.

"Nope," he said. "Not there, either." He reached out, touched her chin with a finger and turned her face back to his. "Haven't needed them in a long time," he said softly.

She knew what he was saying. Believed it. Because Jamie had never lied to her. The only lying that had happened between them was her to herself.

"Besides," he added, "no bed."

"Not that we ever needed one, but you might need to fix that," she answered, reaching up to press his hand against her face.

For a moment something shadowed his eyes. "Don't want me in yours?"

Swiftly she moved both her hands to cup his face, so he couldn't turn away. "What I don't want," she said, "is all of Whiskey River having a gossip fest about us."

She saw him process it, that her place was just a couple of blocks from the town square, and people came to do business in the Mahan Services office if nothing else. Then he smiled ruefully. "And they would, wouldn't they?"

"Childhood sweethearts reunited? You bet they will."

"Are we, Zee? Reunited?"

"Rekindled, at least," she said.

He let out an exaggerated, dramatic sigh. "Then I guess I'd better get moving on that bed."

"And condoms," she suggested, with equal drama.

And suddenly he was laughing, and for that moment he was the old Jamie, her Jamie. "Wonder if there's a place that has both?"

She grinned. "If there's not, there should be. Imagine the sales."

"Imagine if it was here in town," he said dryly.

She widened her eyes. "Martha would strain her voice."

And then they were both laughing, and for that brief moment, the youthful joy in each other was as free and pure as it had ever been.

Chapter Twenty-Seven

"I STILL CAN'T believe you asked him that, and with a straight face!"

Jamie looked at Zee, just to make sure the outrage was mock. She was grinning, so he thought it safe to assume it was. And he grinned back at her.

"Well, we did discuss it."

He wasn't quite sure himself why the question about condoms had popped out in the middle of the furniture store, but something about the older man's expression as he looked at them had done it.

"It was worth it to see the look on his face. And to see him laugh."

"'I have six children,'" Jamie quoted. "'If the store where we bought our bed had offered them, that number might be lower.'"

She laughed, that lovely sound he'd so missed. "Lucky kids."

"Yes." He didn't have to look at her to know they were both thinking the same thing; the parents they had lost. But she had had True, and he Aunt Millie, and they'd both ended up with good lives despite the loss.

"Too bad it won't be delivered until tomorrow," she said.

He glanced at her as he drove. What he saw in her face made his blood heat and surge at the same time, and it was all he could do not to shift uncomfortably in the driver's seat. Damn, she brought him to the boil like no one ever had.

Or ever would.

"Yeah," he muttered, turning back to the road.

He was convinced of that now. Nothing had ever matched what he'd had with Zee. And he wondered, not for the first time, if it had really been worth it. If the success and unexpected recognition the band—and he himself—had gotten was indeed worth what he'd given up. Once he would have said it was worth anything. Now he knew better.

They'd ended up on the outskirts of Austin to make the purchase—both purchases—hoping it was both far enough from Whiskey River to keep the gossip at bay and big enough he wouldn't be recognized. In the end, finding the small, craftsman-run store had solved all the problems plus given him the added pleasure of selecting from some beautiful, handmade pieces. He'd ended up buying not just the big four-poster, but the collection, and a solid, beautifully grained table and chairs for the dining room and a hand-carved, glass-doored cabinet for no other reason than the fanciful dragons on it appealed.

"I've got some cleaning still to do before it gets here," he said when he could trust his voice again.

"I'll help," she said.

"You hate cleaning."

"I expect payment."

"Do you now?" he drawled.

"Indeed, I do," she said, and proceeded to outline exactly what kind of payment she expected.

He stood it for a mile and a half. "If you don't stop," he growled, "I'm going to pull off the road and we'll hit the backseat like the teenagers we were."

"Not necessarily a bad idea," she said blithely, "except the top's down and I think there are laws."

The laugh that burst from him then was like a pressure valve letting go, and he felt better than he had in nearly a year.

ZEE SMOOTHED THE comforter down at the last corner. Abruptly her eyes shifted focus, from the cheerful blue fabric—bluebonnet-blue—to her hand. Her imagination flashed, picturing her hand sliding over his skin. Suddenly she was as overheated as if it were midday midsummer instead of spring. Yet she couldn't seem to stop.

"Never thought I'd envy a piece of material."

His voice came from the doorway behind her and she froze. "Careful," she said, "I might interpret that as an immediate invitation."

She heard a rustling behind her, then footsteps. "Oh, it was," he said huskily.

She turned then, saw that the rustling had been him pulling his shirt over his head and shedding his boots. For a moment she couldn't breathe. He was even more beautiful than he'd been at eighteen. He'd filled out, his shoulders broadened, his chest deeper. But his hips were as narrow, his belly as flat as ever, and he still moved like that barely leashed wild thing. If she'd been any kind of artist, this was what she would pick as her male ideal.

And he looked much, much better than he had when he'd gotten off that plane. Being back in Whiskey River, even for only a short time—God, had it really only been seventeen days?—obviously agreed with him. She hoped she had something to do with that. And marveled at how far they'd come.

Once you quit being a hypocrite.

She shoved the thought aside. They were past that now, and she wasn't going to let it interfere. Not when this man who had always fired her blood was standing here, half-naked and obviously already aroused, in front of her. Not when she was fairly aching to touch him in the old ways, and maybe discover some new ones.

It didn't matter that it was the middle of the day, or that

she had just made the bed for the first time. Nothing mattered except that he was here, and he wanted her. Maybe even as much as she wanted him.

It was familiar, and yet it was brand new.

He hadn't even touched her yet, and she was trembling. And then he did, reaching out to stroke the backs of his fingers over her cheek.

"You're sure, Zee? I don't ever want to hurt you again."

He would stop. She knew that down to her soul, that if she said she was the least bit uncertain, he would stop. For she was suddenly certain that deep down he was still the Jamie Templeton she had loved with all her youthful heart. He might have stumbled along the way, fallen prey to temptations few could resist, but he'd pulled himself out of it.

You know what I used to think when it got really crazy, when I nearly stepped off the edge? I used to think, 'Man, Zee would chew me out for that.' And I stepped back.

So yes, he would stop. And she'd likely slide to the floor right here, an aching puddle of want and need.

"You didn't hurt me," she said, needing to make sure he understood. "I did. By not being honest with myself, or you. You only did what you always said you would do. What I told you to do."

"Tell me what to do now, Zee." His voice was rough, rumbling in that way she remembered so well; it sent chills and heat through her at the same time.

"I think you remember what to do," she said, in a whisper that was all she could manage her throat was so tight with wanting him.

He reached out and tugged at the buttons of her blouse. She saw the barest tremor in his hands, and this proof he was as hungry as she was only kicked up the heat. The blouse fell open and Jamie swallowed visibly.

She couldn't speak at all anymore. But she could touch, and so she reached out and laid her palms flat on his chest. The heat of him seared her, and the low sound he made as skin met skin was the fuel to the fire that had apparently only been banked all this time.

He closed his eyes as she ran her fingers over his chest, then slid down to the ridges of his abdomen. He kept them closed as he went the other direction, slipping his hands up to cup her breasts. The thin, lacy bra was no barrier, and she moaned at the long-missed feel of his hands on her.

His eyes were still closed. That made her the tiniest bit nervous. She reached up and brushed a fingertip over the thick sweep of his eyelashes. "Jamie?"

Something must have been in her voice, because he answered her unspoken question.

"I'm not sure I can handle touching you and looking at you at the same time." But then he did look at her. And when he spoke again, there was such fierceness in his voice it fairly screamed the truth of what he was saying. "I never stopped wanting you, Zee. Never."

The words were like a caress in themselves. And then his thumbs brushed over her nipples and a moan escaped her as the darting fire woke up every nerve. The silky blouse slid off her shoulders, and he reached behind her. He fumbled with the clasp of her bra, but after a moment dropped his forehead to rest on hers.

"I can't. My hands are shaking."

The admission tipped her over the edge. She reached back and undid the clasp herself. Jamie tugged the fabric away, and she saw that indeed his hands were shaking when he reached to again cup her breasts, skin to skin again, and her body cramped with need. Only him, only this man had ever been able to spark this conflagration in her so high, so fast.

He lifted her breasts at the same moment he lowered his head. He caught one already tight nipple in his mouth, teased it with his tongue. She arched to him, a sharp cry breaking from her. He repeated the action on the other, then suckled her deeply. She clutched at him, felt the power in his arms, his shoulders, which only made her treasure more that moment of admission that his hands were shaking. Because he wanted her that much.

She reached for the snap of his jeans, wanting him naked against her more than she wanted her next breath. She was barely aware of him pulling at her own clothes, didn't care as long as she got his off.

He was more beautiful than she remembered. Or it was

the change in him, from youth to full manhood. But it didn't matter, because everything came flooding back to her, all the things she'd tried not to think of for so long, the way he liked to be touched, the spots that had made him gasp, groan, or let her name out in reverence. And she wanted to hit them all, but he was touching her, caressing her, and it was clear he remembered just as well as she did.

They went down to the bed in a tangle. Wrestled with the condom. And then she was kissing, licking, tasting every bit of him she could reach, and he was doing the same. The flames burned hotter, until she was clawing at him, begging him to hurry. She wrapped her legs around his lean hips, reaching between them to stroke the rigid length of him. She simply could not wait to feel him, every inch of him, inside her again.

The first blunt probing told her how ready she was, for he slid easily over slick flesh. Then he stopped, and she nearly cried out.

"Don't stop," she pleaded.

"Not stopping. Savoring. Every. Damned. Bit. Of. You."

It came out in gasping chunks of sound, and with every word he slid in a little deeper. And then, with a final fierce thrust, he drove home the rest of the way and she cried out with the sheer, exquisite pleasure of it.

"Zee." He let it out on a harsh breath. "I can't…"

He didn't finish. He tightened his hold on her and began to move. She wanted it to go on forever, but her long-deprived body had other ideas and was gathering itself by his third stroke. Her fingers dug into his back as she clung to him, arching to his thrusts. She felt the moment when he grew even harder, stretching her further, heard him groan low and deep, knew she could let go. And then it was upon her, that flooding wash of pure sensation, and she cried out his name on wave after wave of it. Her name ripped from him and she felt the hot pulse of him inside her, in the moment before he collapsed atop her, panting, but still holding on to her as if for his life.

And for the first time since he'd gone, her life felt whole again.

Chapter Twenty-Eight

STILL HALF ASLEEP, Jamie didn't want to open his eyes. What if it had all been some wishful, longing-induced lustful dream? It had to have been. It was dark now, and the dream had been in daylight. Lovely, sunny daylight, lighting Zee's incredible eyes, gilding her gorgeous body as they came together time after time. That incredible, never matched feeling of sliding into her, that combination of knowing and instinct that intensified every touch, every move, and—

A movement beside him. The slide of a long, sleek leg over his.

Zee.

It was real.

He snapped awake with a jolt. She was watching him. He could see the faint glint of moonlight in her eyes. Those amazing eyes that had gone all hot and soft for him.

"Not sure how to take that you're so surprised," she said. "Not used to waking up with who you went to bed with?" He winced, but before he could speak, she shook her head. "Sorry. That was...reflex. If I really believed that, I wouldn't be here."

"I know that. And for the record, what I'm not used to is waking up with anyone."

"And I know that. Because you told me, and you've never lied to me."

Except lies of omission?

He shoved away the thought. It was getting harder to do each time. And the effort made him seize on another truth, one he could give her. "I was surprised because...I thought it had been a dream. Again."

She went very still. "Again?"

He reached out, brushed a strand of dark hair with his fingers. "Again. And again and again and again."

She stared at him. She wasn't frowning, but she looked...almost confused, which was a rare enough state for Zee Mahan that it put him on alert.

"But you didn't come home," she said softly, and he could tell she was speaking carefully by the way there was not an ounce of her old accusation in her voice.

"I should have. Screw the momentum, the shows every night. I should have come back. At least to see you." He took a deep breath. "And I should have realized when you told me to go you didn't really—"

He stopped when she put a finger to his lips. "That's the crazy part. I did mean it. Your talent, you couldn't just ignore it. I knew you could make it, and I wanted you to. I wanted the world to know your music. It wasn't your fault I couldn't let go of…how I felt about you."

"Does that mean…you still feel it?" He couldn't help how hopeful…or maybe wistful, he sounded.

"It's not…the same," she said, sounding as if she were still choosing her words carefully.

"We're not kids anymore."

She arched a dark brow at him then. "Oh? You seem to have the same…stamina."

She caught him off guard with the humor, and the sound he made was somewhere between a laugh and a cough. "Thanks," he finally managed to get out. "Although I think you may have worn me out."

"I'm not so all fired sure of that," she said, exaggerating the Texas in her voice. "I think it's going to require further testing."

She moved then, running her hands over him in that way that made him suck in a breath so sharply it sounded like a gasp. Maybe it was. She replaced her hands with her mouth, until he thought every muscle in his body was rippling under her luscious kisses.

And then she slid a hand down his belly and found flesh that had been hardened since the moment he'd realized she was really here, that it hadn't been a dream, and he swore under his breath as she curled her fingers around him and stroked.

She kept going until he couldn't stop himself from reaching for her, needing her as hungrily as if it had been the first time. But she pushed him back, gently but with determination, and when she moved to straddle him he gave up the fight happily. And when she guided him into her, until she was holding all of him in that sweet, hot, slick grasp, he gasped out her name. Looking up at her like this again made him feel things he had no name for.

"Have you dreamed of this?" Her voice was barely a whisper.

It was all he could do to speak coherently. "You, riding me? More times than I can count."

"Me, too."

His entire body seemed to knot up at her quiet words. But then she started to move and coherency fled, along with any thought except what this felt like, the rightness of it, the feeling of a long-torn soul mended again. He was burning inside, and there was only one way to save himself. And when he felt it begin for her, felt the clenching of her body around him, he let go and poured himself into her until the fire eased.

Zee had saved him again.

ZEE COULDN'T STOP smiling. It didn't even matter to her that everybody in town was smiling back in that very knowing way she would normally find annoying. She didn't care. She was deliriously happy, and didn't care who knew it. She supposed there were some who thought her a fool for picking up again with the man who'd left her behind, but they didn't know the whole story so she ignored them. To those who asked, with obvious concern, if she knew what she was doing, she simply smiled even wider and said, "Yes."

True never asked. The closest he'd come was the first night she hadn't come home and he'd texted her.

OK?

Very

Then, after a pause, *Jamie?*

Perfect.

He'd sent an emoji with its tongue hanging out, and never said another word about it, just accepted. She loved her brother more than ever.

It had been the most glorious week of her life, she thought as she pulled off the highway toward the Whiskey River rescue facility. Kelsey was there, working with Shadow, the latest arrival. Only Kelsey, she thought, would be here two days before her wedding.

The little black gelding had filled out, his coat now sleek and shining in the sun, but that wasn't the biggest difference. The biggest change was his attitude; the spooky, terrified, abused horse he'd been was long gone, and he was the sweet-natured creature he'd been meant to be.

When Kelsey walked the horse over, Zee held out the envelope holding the finalized details of the schedule for Saturday. She knew Kelsey's mom was flying in this afternoon, and Deck's agent and attorney, who had told her when she'd made the arrangements that they were delighted to stand in for the family Deck didn't have.

"Somebody's going to snap him up," Zee said with a grin as she leaned on the corral fence.

"If I can let him go," Kelsey answered as she took it. The horse, who once would have shied at the big tan thing that made a scary rustling sound, merely looked at it, sniffed, decided it wasn't of interest and nudged Kelsey for a pat. "He's so good with the outreach kids, we may just have to keep him."

"Any excuse in a storm," Zee teased.

"Absolutely," Kelsey grinned back. "So how's Jamie?"

Perfect. "Fine."

"I'm really glad about you two."

"My brother been chatting?"

Kelsey laughed. "You know he wouldn't. And he didn't have to. It's written all over your face."

"So you don't think I'm crazy?"

Kelsey leaned back a little, still smiling, and arched a brow at her. "Girlfriend, I've *seen* the man. I think you'd be crazy not to."

"Can't argue that," Zee said, "but..." Her voice trailed off. She wasn't sure what she wanted to say, wasn't even sure what she was feeling.

"It's more than that," Kelsey said. "There's a connection between you. True says it's been that way since you were kids."

Zee nodded. "It started when our folks were killed, but...even then it was more than that."

Kelsey nodded in turn. "He's a good guy, Zee. And I'm not just saying that because he and Deck hit it off, which is no small thing." She gestured over her shoulder at the horse behind her. "Shadow likes him, and he's a pretty darn good judge of people. He's had to be."

Zee blinked. "Jamie's been here?"

"A couple of times, since he's been back. He's good with all of the horses, but Shadow really took to him." Kelsey grinned again. "And Jamie never blinked when I put him to work."

"I'm amazed he still had the energy, with all he's been doing at the house. But he was never afraid of hard work."

"He hasn't been here for about a week, though." That grin again. "I think he found something better to do."

It suddenly hit her. Kelsey's grin. True's grin. And Deck, and Hope. That expression of utter happiness that she was so glad to see and yet that had sparked a near-painful emptiness in her.

She'd been looking at that grin in the mirror for days and hadn't even realized it.

"The difference is obvious in both of you. It's amazing. Whatever problems there were or are," Kelsey said, her voice and expression serious now, "it's worth working out."

"I'll take that as advice from an expert in doing just

that," Zee said. And she meant it; the walls Kelsey had had to batter down to reach Deck had been beyond formidable.

"Do. You make each other so clearly happy."

"I hope we're half as happy as you guys are."

And when she got back in her car, she couldn't resist looking in the rearview mirror.

Yep, it was the same grin.

Chapter Twenty-Nine

ZEE SMILED AT Hope's expression of awe as she looked around at the decorated pavilion. Sweet, ethereal music, from a harp and flute duo Kelsey had asked for after hearing them in Kerrville last year, floated out from the speakers.

"Your fiancé's pretty darned amazing, isn't he?" she said.

"He is. The pavilion's gorgeous, but you, too," Hope said. "The way the fabric flows down all the columns and drapes in-between, and everything looks so…together!"

Zee nodded in satisfaction. It had turned out well. "Bluebonnet-blue," she murmured. "Too bad we're a month too late for the real thing; that would have been beautiful."

"I just saw Kelsey. I don't think she cares."

Zee grinned. "She is pretty happy, isn't she?"

Hope looked at her consideringly. Then, in carefully even tones, she asked, "So are you. How's Jamie?"

Zee fluttered her eyelashes exaggeratedly to match her drawl. "Whyever did you connect those two things?"

Hope laughed. Zee was glad to hear it; her future sister-in-law had changed so much in the past four months. Not as much as today's groom, but she hadn't started in quite that awful a place.

"Actually," she said, answering seriously now, "he's nervous."

Hope looked startled. "Nervous? The guy who performs in front of thousands?"

"Crazy, huh? Only one song, and he's a wreck. It's Deck and Kelsey. Plus he's never sung at a wedding before, and he knows most of the people coming, so it's…different."

"That's sweet," Hope said. "That he cares so much."

Yes, it was. And no one knew better than she did how much Jamie Templeton was capable of caring, because over the last week he'd proven it again and again.

In the end, everything came together beautifully, thanks to True's preparations and Zee's planning. It was a small—at least, given Deck's worldwide fame—wedding, but everyone there had a direct link to the couple who were about to make the most public and heartfelt declaration of the love they'd unexpectedly found.

Zee knew many of the attendees, for she and Kelsey had friends in common in Whiskey River. She met Deck's agent who had flown in from New York, and his attorney, who happened to be the father of one of his biggest young fans, which was how they'd connected. And that boy, who was so excited at being invited he could hardly sit still. Former recluse that he was, his guest list had been slim, mostly people connected to his work, but he'd brushed it off.

"This is for Kels," he'd said.

Zee spotted her brother—the best man—tall and lean and quite striking in the simple, classic tux. And she smiled. "He does clean up nice, doesn't he?"

"Oh, yes," Hope said fervently, and Zee guessed she knew why they had almost run late this morning.

"I'm glad to see Kelsey's dad's friends here," Zee said, looking at the group of men taking seats to her right, several of them in military uniform. Eric Blaine had died in action years ago, but clearly he had been liked and respected. And his family had not been forgotten.

"You don't forget your brothers-in-arms."

The deep, male, very Texan voice came from behind her. She saw Hope smile in the moment before she turned to see Jack Ducane, in formal wear that had a distinctly Texan air—pearl snaps instead of buttons, a string tie, and the arrowed yoke—as befitted his status as a Texas Ranger. She was glad to see Hope's smile was genuine, for she had spent a long time being wary of any law enforcement types. But Jack had helped her, and had managed to earn the hard-won trust of Deck as well, a testament to his rock-solid integrity.

Jack had also hand-picked some security to keep the media who had somehow—Zee suspected Martha—learned of the ceremony today, clustered outside the gate.

"Thanks for keeping the hounds at bay," she said to him now.

"Glad to help," Jack said. He looked at Hope. "That's

twice this year I've been able to do something cheerful."

Hope looked startled, but she smiled. Zee thought it was grimly indicative of what Jack usually dealt with that he thought helping someone get through an ugly murder trial cheerful.

"Your tie matches the trimmings," Zee said. The neatly tied strip of blue fabric was almost exactly the same shade as the draped fabric and the table embellishments.

"And Kelsey's mom's dress," Hope said, looking at the matron of honor.

To Zee's surprise, Jack looked uncomfortable.

"She's as beautiful as her daughter," Zee said.

"Yes. Yes, she is," Jack said, and something in his voice tripped Zee's radar. She filed it away on her list of things to be considered later.

The music changed, a clear signal, and everyone took their seats. True took his spot up front, and a moment later, a clearly nervous Deck joined him. True grabbed his shoulder and grinned at him, and even from here Zee could almost feel the tension break. Bless her brother, he always knew.

The ceremony was the most wonderful combination of tradition and unique touches Zee had ever seen. Kelsey, glowing in a gown that gleamed like snow under the spring sun, covered the distance from the house to the pavilion, on a big gray horse. She wondered briefly how women had ever ridden like that, sidesaddle, but Kelsey—and Granite—were clearly in tune; the horse was moving with delicate care, almost prancing, as if he understood this was somehow special.

The moment Deck saw her, his entire expression and demeanor changed. The nervousness vanished, to be replaced with an awed love Zee doubted he would ever lose. And in that moment, she thought Declan Kilcoyne the bravest man she'd ever met.

Hope, sitting next to her—on the outer edge, so Zee could deal with anything that went amiss—asked, "Who is that?" when a tall, gray-haired man in uniform held his hand up to help Kelsey slide off the horse and began to walk with her down the aisle. An aisle lined with another man in uniform every few feet along the way.

"He was her father's commanding officer," Zee said, her throat a little tight. "And they all served with him."

Hope sucked in an audible breath, and Zee saw her hand go to her lips as if to hold back a sound.

"Me, too," Zee said, blinking rapidly for a moment.

The stern-faced officer handed Kelsey off to Deck, whispering something that made them both smile. Then he turned to the woman who was the model for the bride, and with an old-world sort of courtly grace, he took her hand and bowed over it. Lisa Blaine colored slightly, and Zee saw her make a quick swipe at her eyes. Even not knowing what was said she felt her own eyes sting a little again.

The stir in the crowd warned her. She looked up, and

Jamie was there, taking the stool beside the microphone, slinging that sweet old guitar Aunt Millie had bought him all those years ago around in front.

He said simply, "This is for Kelsey and Declan." Not another word, although it was obvious many had recognized him. But she knew he'd decided that long ago; this was for Deck and Kelsey, and Jamie wasn't about to distract from that.

She recognized the delicate picking out of individual notes the moment he began. *Morning.* It was one of her favorites, a paean to the sun's rising after a stormy night. He'd told her the couple had chosen the song because the sentiment had special meaning to them.

It began quietly, Jamie's voice little more than a whisper. But it built as if it were the rising sun itself, dancing over the intricate melody, soaring to a triumphant and beautiful sort of power that took her breath away.

She hadn't heard him sing live in so long. It brought tears to her eyes now; his voice had always seemed a miracle to her, but she'd forgotten how incredible it was to hear him pour himself into it like this. Whatever had been bothering him that day when she'd heard him playing, he'd obviously set it aside. This was for his friends, and they got his all.

She didn't know what the protocol was for a wedding singer, but if it wasn't standing up and applauding, everyone broke it.

He came to her when he was done, and she hugged him.

"Look at them," she whispered to him, nodding at Kelsey and Deck. "That was the best present you could give them, next to being here."

"Kelsey is pure sunshine, and Deck…gives me hope."

There was a touch of it there, in his voice, whatever was eating at him, but it vanished as the officiator began.

Much later, when there was finally nothing left but the cleanup, Hope looked around at the debris. The guests had been tidy enough, but there was a lot of trash in the bins and crumbs on the floor of the pavilion. She gave True a sideways look. "Can we elope?"

True, his best man duties discharged in full with Kelsey and Deck off to places unknown, laughed and hugged her.

"This is nothing, for Mahan Services," Zee said airily, and dug in, heedless of her silky blue dress and high heels.

"Especially now that we can add horse caretaking to the résumé," True said. He glanced at Jamie. "With some help," he added.

Zee stopped, looking at Jamie in some surprise; he hadn't mentioned this. He shrugged. "I told Kelsey I'd stop by and spend some time with them. It's important to be consistent, to get the ones that were abused trusting people again."

Zee smiled at him, feeling a kernel of warmth expanding inside her at this evidence Jamie was rebuilding a place for himself in Whiskey River. A little afraid of what might be showing in her face, she turned and grabbed the broom True had brought from his truck. He and Hope went to the other side of the pavilion and began to fold up the chairs and stack them for pickup.

"Leave the crumbs," Jamie suggested as he watched her with the broom. "Give the field mice a treat."

After learning that he'd offered to look after Kelsey's horses, and since he had jumped in and was helping in the cleanup—and wouldn't Ms. L.A. glamour love that?—she gave the suggestion strong consideration. "I'll sweep them off the edge, leave them there," she said.

Jamie went back to gathering trash and stuffing it into the big, heavy trash bags True usually used on construction sites. "Have I mentioned how beautiful you look?" Jamie asked as he knotted the top of one of the bags.

"Not since this morning," she said with a smile.

His gaze went suddenly hot, and Zee remembered with a flash of echoing heat that Jamie hadn't only said she looked beautiful when she'd finished dressing for the day, he'd said it when she'd been astride him in the early morning light, savoring the feel of his rigid flesh stretching her with slow, undulating movements.

"Hold that thought," he whispered to her.

"Oh, I will," she whispered back. And looked forward to tonight, when she could do more than think about it.

⭐

"Jamie?"

Zee, whispering his name into the darkness, her long, sleek, naked body pressed to his. In her bed tonight, simply because they'd come here for her to change.

It was something he'd dreamed about so often in the years he'd been gone. And now she was here, in his arms, both of them sated, tension banished. It was more incredible than it had ever been, and in those moments of joy he dared to hope that maybe, just maybe, they could rebuild something great on the foundation of what they'd had before.

Until he faced yet again that he was lying to her. That he hadn't told her the real reason that had sent him running home to her, as if she were still the muse of his youth, as if he had the right to expect her to fix what was wrong with him. Without even telling her what it was.

"What is it? What's wrong? I know something is."

"Ah, Zee," he said, the vast ache inside creeping into his voice. "You always know, don't you?"

"Jamie," she said again, sitting up now, worry a ragged undertone in her words. "I know there's something, there's been something, for a long time. Since even before Derek. Hasn't there."

It wasn't really a question, so he didn't answer. He closed his eyes, as if the darkness of the night alone wasn't enough of a buffer between him and the reality, and the moment that was finally here.

"Tell me. Please."

"I...can't."

She was very quiet for a moment before she said, "Can't? Or won't?"

"If I tell you, if I put it into words, especially to you...then it's real."

"It's that bad?"

His mouth tightened. He let out a suppressed breath. "To the state of the world, hardly."

"I don't care about the state of the world right now. I care about you."

"I know. God, I know." His voice broke, and he turned to her. He couldn't stop himself, he shivered in her arms. He was on the edge—that sharp, slicing edge—and he could feel it starting to cut, could feel the bleeding start.

She tightened her arms around him. "It'll be all right. Whatever it is, we'll fight it, fix it, get past it."

She sounded scared. And he'd done that to her.

"Zee, I'm sorry, I—"

"I'm not going to lose you again, Jamie Templeton. So whatever it is, you just hang on." She hugged him fiercely this time. "And someday you'll write a song about it, and that will be all that's left of it."

A harsh, choking sound broke from him. And the dam broke within, and he couldn't hold it back.

"There won't be another song. Ever."

"Jamie?"

He made one last try to stop it, but failed. The truth

came ripping from him. "It's gone."

"What's gone?"

"The music, Zee. It's gone."

Chapter Thirty

ZEE FELT ANOTHER tremor go through him. She held on, trying to process what he'd said.

"Gone?"

In the dark she felt more than saw him nod.

"What, exactly," she said carefully, "do you mean?"

"It's just not there."

"How can you say that, after the wedding? That was the most incredible—"

"Old."

"What?"

"That was an old song. Already written."

"Jamie—"

It came out in a rush then. "Every time I try for something new, it comes out just a variation on an old one. Music, lyrics, doesn't matter. It's gone."

"No, it can't be," she said soothingly. "It's as much a part of you as those green eyes."

"It always was. Now there's just this…hollow place inside. Like I've been scoured out."

She was sitting up now, looking down at him. In the dim light she could see only the faint gleam of the blond streaks in his hair, the shape of his jaw. But she could tell that jaw was clenched. He was fighting for…something. To tell her more? To not tell her more?

"This has…never happened before?"

"Not like this. I'd feel dry sometimes, but there were places I could go and just sit and soak in the world, and eventually it would come out as music. And if that didn't do it, there were things I could do, like go to the beach, or for a long drive."

"Or a batting cage?" she said, trying to lighten this up, trying to make it anything but what he seemed to be saying it was. And it was true. Jamie had been a star baseball player in school. Some thought that would be the career he pursued. But then the music had called, and he had never looked back.

"Tried," he admitted. "Everything, Zee. I've tried everything that has ever worked, and nothing."

The old Zee, the one who had been angry with him, would have asked if that was the real reason he'd come home. But now all she could hear was the agony in his voice and the thought barely formed before it was smashed and discarded. It didn't matter, even if it was true.

Besides, there was no room for it, because her own horror at what he was saying was rising within her. Jamie, without his music? No more of those tunes that made you want to dance, no more driving anthems that made your pulse race, no more lilting melodies that made you wonder how a piece of music you'd never heard before could make your heart soar?

"All right," she said slowly, "so you drained the well dry, and maybe Derek put the lid on it. That doesn't mean it won't refill again."

He shook his head, his eyes closing as if the pain was physical as well. "I haven't written a new song in nearly a year."

She didn't know what to say. She knew that every season's touring usually included several new songs. Some instantly took off, embraced by fans and with concert videos posted practically before they got off stage. Others didn't and were discarded, although it seemed every song had devotees—some just had a smaller number.

She remembered asking him once, toward the beginning when she'd been amazed by his productivity, where it all came from. He'd told her he didn't know, but that sometimes the pressure inside got so big that he had to open the tap for a while, or he'd burst. But for him, to go a year without producing anything was akin to the river running dry. Whiskey River sometimes ran low, sometimes in a dry year down to a trickle, but it never, ever ran dry.

But Jamie apparently had.

"Jamie—"

"Derek dying was what made me face it. I did a good job

lying to myself up until then. Pretending it was just temporary. But at his funeral I realized the music was as dead as he was."

She needed time to think about this, painful as it was. There had to be something to do about it, she just needed to figure it out. Because a world without his music was not a place she wanted to be.

"We'll figure it out," she whispered. "There's an answer, we just need to find it."

And since she didn't know what else to do right now she simply held him, until the warmth of their closeness blossomed into heat. And then she made love to him, slow, sweet, lingering over every spot she knew made him gasp or writhe, stroking, kissing, tasting, until there was room for nothing in his mind but her and how she was making him feel.

She began it with every intention of driving all else out of his mind, and it ended with both of them nearly screaming with the intensity of it. And when he came with a rough shout of her name, she held him within her as if that alone could heal the hole within him.

ZEE WENT INTO the office, her mind preoccupied with what Jamie had told her. He'd gone back to Aunt Millie's, she suspected because working like a fiend took his mind off of it. She realized she hadn't made coffee, went back to the kitchen. She was working by rote, going through the motions. She'd done it while half-asleep enough times that doing it while utterly distracted was nothing.

He'd meant it. She could sense it. That he was utterly convinced this was more than just a block. That the gift that had always lived in his soul was truly gone. When he'd left her this morning, she'd been hesitant to let him go alone. She'd already warned him not to even think about shutting her out now that he'd told her, because she'd known from his expression that his thoughts were veering that way.

She poured her first cup with an automatic motion. Picked it up and headed for the office as she reminded herself of what Deck had told her, about different ways of dealing. And Jamie's way was clearly much closer to that of the famous writer than to her own, she thought as she hit the switch on her computer. And so she'd let him go, with the warning that she'd be checking on him. And she would, as soon as she finished—

Jamie's voice echoed through the office. She realized she had automatically put her phone in the sound system and begun her play list, because she always did. For a moment she stood frozen, the sweet, innocent love song made impossibly, achingly beautiful by the power and emotion of that voice swamping her. Memories of nights in his arms tangled with the ache this song always roused in her and then twisted into some hard, tight knot of anguish at the thought that maybe he was right. The idea that there would be no more of this, no more music like this, with the power to stop people in their tracks, make them cry or smile or dance or sing along even if they had the voice of a Texas mule was...

Unacceptable. Utterly and totally unacceptable.

No matter how she'd felt about him, justified or not, Zee had ever and always loved Jamie's music. She loved the way he turned an everyday phrase into a refrain that tugged at the heart. She loved the way he tweaked the melody just a bit from what might be expected, throwing in a minor chord to reframe the chorus from the rest. She loved the way his playing went from hard and pounding to so light and ethereal it didn't seem possible it was the same instrument.

And most of all she loved his voice, the most amazing instrument of all, and the way it could go from choirboy pure and light to achingly full of longing to rough and low and downright sexy. And the way he had sounded at the wedding, full of the emotion that made his songs burrow into people's hearts.

A shiver went through her and she wrapped her arms around herself at the thought of losing that. There would always be the music he'd already done, but no more new songs? No excitement at the release of a new one, no happy wondering what his clever mind and nimble fingers and agile voice would combine to produce next?

Definitely unacceptable.

And when she thought of what such a loss would do to

him, how entwined with his very identity his music was, she fairly ached with the pain of it, for him. So much she couldn't bear it. She had to do something.

She turned on her heel and walked to the door to True's side of the house. For years he would have been gone by now, well into a long, hard workday, but that had changed, along with many other things, with Hope. He called out a "Come on in," and she opened the door.

Despite her inner turmoil, she paused for a moment to enjoy the sight of her brother and Hope in a close embrace in the kitchen next to the open dishwasher. "Aren't you two domesticated," she teased.

"I'm just glad to have dishes to clean," Hope said.

"And I'm glad to let her," True said with a grin. "For now. What's up?"

"Where do we stand, work wise?"

"Pretty much done." True gave her a slightly embarrassed smile. "Now that the wedding's over, I thought I'd take a few days off. Except for looking in at the rescue, of course."

Zee grinned at him, and it wasn't just because he'd just solved her problem for her, as he so often did. "A vacation? True Mahan is actually going to take a vacation? The world may stop turning."

"Yeah, yeah," her brother said, grinning back now. "Why? Somebody call with a job?"

"Nothing urgent, just a couple of requests for estimates. I

put them off until after the wedding anyway." She hesitated, then went on. "I wanted some time off, too."

"Can't imagine why," True said, still grinning.

"That, too," Zee admitted.

"But there's more, isn't there?" Hope said. Zee didn't know if it was her experience of being on the run for so long or if she was just a quick study, but her future sister-in-law had learned to read her pretty well. "Jamie? What's eating at him?"

"Yes."

Silence spun out for a moment. Then True spoke, softly. "Take whatever time you—and he—need. If anyone can help him get past whatever it is, it's you."

She hoped he was right.

Chapter Thirty-One

"I WAS THINKING," Zee said.

Jamie looked up. "When are you not?"

"If you wanted a mindless female, you—"

"Came to the wrong place," he finished the old mantra for her, making sure she saw he was smiling. Then he added, "More than ever now."

He went back to the cabinet door he was fastening. He'd been checking on Kelsey's horses in the mornings, and working on this in the afternoons. He'd stripped the kitchen cabinets and repainted them a bright white, and was just now putting the doors back on. It had been a lot of work, but a lot of work was what he wanted right now. What he needed.

Well, that and the passion-filled nights with Zee. Those, he thought, could get him through damn near anything. Just as they had years ago. He had…not forgotten, but time and distance had clouded the memories a bit, of how cracklingly, vividly alive she was, and made him feel when they were together. Especially in those hot, fevered moments in the

Texas night.

"I want to make one suggestion," she said, not looking at him, "and then you can go back to wrestling on your own. Will you listen?"

Damn. He thought she'd been awfully quiet about it since he'd poured his guts out to her the night after the wedding. They'd worked on the house side by side day after day, and she'd never brought it up. He hadn't talked about it since, although he couldn't deny the pressure relief telling her had given him. It didn't make the weight of it any less. It was only that he'd shared it. He'd forgotten how she could do that for him, but he remembered now.

And she'd gone a week and a half. A record for Zee, when she had something in her teeth.

He tightened the last screw, checked that the door swung easily and silently, then straightened. He turned around. She had the last door on the small kitchen table, and was replacing the hardware.

She was, he realized, waiting for an answer. That was a change, he registered. But then, she usually, at least before, wouldn't have even asked, she would have just said what she wanted to say. So she was being careful. Whether it was because of what he'd told her, or just general tentativeness because they'd rekindled…them, he didn't know.

"You're at the top of my list of people I'll listen to," he said.

She looked up then. She was smiling, and he knew he'd

somehow found the right thing to say. "Short list?"

He grinned. "Very."

Her smile widened, but when she spoke her voice was quiet, serious. "Later, when they're back and when you're ready…talk to Deck."

He blinked. "What?"

"Who better to understand what you're going through?"

He stared at her. "Deck?" The guy was a freaking genius, his books so intricate and smooth and engrossing that Jamie couldn't imagine him ever stumbling. "I can't imagine he ever—"

She held up a hand. He stopped. "That bad place he was in when Kelsey first met him? Part of it was he was completely blocked on the last book."

He hadn't known. He'd thought it was mainly Deck's past Kelsey had had to fight through. "He was?" he said, rather inanely.

"It was so bad he was going to kill off Sam."

Jamie's breath caught. He really hadn't known that. Kill off his boy hero, the main character beloved by millions?

"So when you feel you can, talk to him, will you?"

He wasn't sure he could. Then again, who better to understand than someone who'd been there?

"Maybe."

"He might have some real answers."

"Maybe," he said again. He never would have thought of it on his own. Maybe he had some walls of his own to batter down. He hefted the screwdriver in his hand, tapped at the bright red handle as he considered. "Maybe," he repeated a third time, with more emphasis, thinking he might really do it.

"Do. I can only give support," she said softly. "And tell you that the only thing I love more than your music is you."

That blasted all other thoughts out of his head. She'd said it. She'd actually said it, that she loved him. And done it as casually as if it were a given, and had been all along.

"Zee…"

It was all he could get out. Something had exploded in his gut, leaving him hot and cold and shivery all at the same time. And had the strangest feeling that if he let out what was jammed up in his throat it would be some kind of primal howl.

And then he thought how very Zee this was, to pick this moment, when they were in the middle of paint and sawdust and scattered tools, a very matter-of-fact moment to say matter-of-factly the one thing he'd never dared hope to hear again.

Because he couldn't speak he went to her, pulled her into his arms. He simply held her, until his throat loosened enough to where he could get the words out.

"I love you, Zee. I never stopped. I just got…lost for a while."

"I know," she whispered.

And later they found themselves showering off sawdust

that had wound up in some interesting places.

⭐

"WELL, YOU LOOK disgustingly happy," Jamie teased.

Deck grinned at him. "I didn't even know this happy existed."

Clearly the two-week honeymoon on some private island had agreed with the new Mr. and Mrs. Kilcoyne. "I'm glad for you, man."

"I know." Deck eyed him knowingly. "You're looking a bit happier yourself."

"I am," Jamie said, then hesitated.

"But?"

He let out a breath. He didn't really think anybody could help him. But if anyone could, it might just be this man.

Besides, he'd promised Zee.

Once he started, it came out easily, either because he'd already told Zee, or because he was barely two sentences into it before Deck was nodding understandingly.

"Been there, my friend," Deck said when he'd finished, "and it sucks in a very, very big way."

"Yeah. But you got through it."

"Thanks to Kelsey," Deck said. "But she says I had to be ready to hear it first."

"How'd you do that?"

"Not consciously, so I don't know if it would work intentionally done that way," Deck said. "I can only tell you how it happened."

"Desperate," Jamie said dryly. "Shoot."

Deck shrugged. "I started thinking of it as over. Cut it out of my life, tried to cut it out of my mind." He grimaced. "I think cutting off a finger would have been easier."

"I get that," Jamie muttered. He already felt like something crucial had been amputated.

"I kept telling myself I was done. That I'd had unexpected success and I should be glad I'd had even that. That I should figure out what I'd do with myself now that I wasn't writing anymore. I had enough money, so that wasn't a worry. So I worked around here," he said, gesturing at the house and the garden that was a green oasis even in the brown of an early Texas summer. "Ran a lot. Swam a lot. Until I was so exhausted I could hardly move. Tried to get too tired to think."

"Did that work? Because it sure as hell hasn't for me."

"No. But at the same time I told myself I was doing it because I wasn't a writer anymore. I was done. Past. And that, I think, got me to where I was…open when Kelsey came up with the answer. To where I could see the answer when it finally came. Before I think I would have just batted it away like everything else."

Jamie thought about what his friend had said as he drove back to the house. The Mustang tooled along smoothly, and he focused on the wind in his hair and the sun on his shoulders. This wasn't a bad life, not really. Like Deck he had enough money to live comfortably for a long time, if not luxuriously. But he didn't need luxury. Not if he had Zee.

But it was a couple of days of turning it over in his mind before he could actually formulate the thought. Zee kept to her word, and neither said nor asked anything about it. It was as if she could sense his inner battle and left him to fight it, while still being almost always within reach. It was exactly the kind of support he needed, and that she'd realized it, that this was the way he had to do it, told him just how much she'd meant that apology. And that promise.

And that she loved him.

He clung to that memory as he fought through the automatic protest of his mind. His own personal identity had been wrapped up in his music for so long, it was like trying to accept that his eyes had changed color. Finally he reduced it down to the essentials.

Just write it off. Count the years with Scorpions as a success. Do something else. He'd been a musician, now he wasn't. Simple, really.

And yet the hardest thing in the world.

Could he really do it? How long before the need to keep trying, to keep testing that dead, empty place where the music used to live inside him faded? It had been a year now. But he hadn't given up, hadn't consciously quit. But did it even count as quitting if he was doing it in the hopes of the same kind of rescue Deck had gotten? And who was supposed to do it? Zee? She'd already done so much for him.

He thought of what Deck had said. Maybe he needed to cut off that finger. That'd do it, if he chose a critical one. No guitar picking then.

He nearly laughed at himself when he realized what he was thinking. Desperate wasn't even the word.

Then one afternoon he was up on the roof, clearing debris out of a rain gutter, when Zee's car pulled into the drive. She'd had some work to do now that True was slowly gearing back up again. She parked next to the Mustang, and it made him grin again to see the clash of colors.

Or because she'd admitted finally that she probably had chosen that color because it matched his eyes. Those nights were the only thing helping him hang on.

And in that moment she looked around, as if searching for something. She spotted him as he dropped down from the roof, and her smile lit her face. And his heart.

And in that moment he realized he could do it, if he had to. Because she would be enough. As long as he had Zee he could deal with the rest, whatever it was. Or wasn't.

THE FIRST TIME she heard him say it, casually, Zee nearly stopped breathing.

It had been a simple exchange with Charlie, who had just

delivered the new outdoor table and chairs Jamie had bought to replace the ones that had disappeared. She'd been happily planning the barbecue he'd suggested they have here this summer when she'd come around the corner just in time to hear them talking.

"Are you going to put together a new band?"

"No. I'm done."

"But—"

"I've had my run. It was fun while it lasted. You got the other chairs, right?"

She dodged back around the corner of the house, out of his sight. She felt as if she'd been stabbed, the pain was so sharp. She could only imagine how it felt to him, to believe it enough to actually say it so offhandedly.

It took her until late that night, when they were wrapped in each other, to work up to asking him about it.

"Of course it hurts," he said flatly. "But that doesn't change it."

She kissed him. "I'm sorry. It just sounded so...matter-of-fact when you said it."

"It is a matter of fact. It's gone, I'm done." He sucked in a deep breath, and she heard him let it out slowly. "And saying it like that, to other people, it's all part of convincing my head of what my heart already knows."

"I love you, Jamie."

He rolled over, pulled her to him. "I know. That's the only thing getting me through."

She made love to him then, intent only on driving every other thought out of his mind. And judging by the way he groaned her name as he erupted into her, she succeeded.

Gradually the newness of him being back in Whiskey River faded. People began to accept, both his presence and the fact that he quietly made clear time and again that he was just plain Jamie Templeton now, the rock star trappings left behind for good. Whatever advice Deck had given him, he'd clearly taken it to heart. But no matter how much she had gained by it, it still hurt Zee's heart a little every time she heard him say it.

And when he one day reached the point where, sitting in the tree house after an afternoon spent revisiting the time when it had been their refuge, he said he needed to figure out what he was going to do with the rest of his life, she knew the process was nearly complete.

"What do you want to do?"

"I don't know." He leaned back on his elbows, gave her a lazy smile she wasn't positive was completely genuine. "Maybe let you support me."

She shrugged. "Fine."

He blinked. "Kidding. I've been careful. There's enough money for quite a while."

"I know." She gave him a sideways look. "But I also know you're far from the type who'd be able to just do nothing."

He lay back down, looking up at the boards above them.

"Maybe I'll build tree houses."

"You'd be good at it."

"And I'd enjoy it."

She smothered the pang. Buried the memory of that man who'd once owned any stage he was on. "That's what matters. And Templeton's Tree Houses has a certain ring to it."

He smiled again, and this one she was certain was real. "It does."

"True could help you get started. He'd know all the suppliers you'd need."

He sat up. Studied her for a moment before he said softly, "That's my Zee. Organizing, practical."

"You forgot one."

"What?"

"Happy. She's very happy."

He reached for her then. "Then I've done my real job."

She couldn't doubt he meant it. The sincerity of it fairly rang in his voice, and echoed in the way he touched her. And she realized in that moment that in fact he'd come a lot further in this process than she herself had, was a lot closer to total acceptance. Perhaps he was even actually there already.

She wasn't so certain she would ever get there.

Chapter Thirty-Two

Zee sleepily reached for him before she even looked at the clock, which for her was an accomplishment. Even in the middle of the night, it was ingrained in her to check the time. But now there was something more important than that.

This had been the most amazing summer of her life. Jamie had been like a different man, not only having apparently finally won the silent battle he'd been fighting, but also having let go of the pain that had been battering him. It had taken a while to finally find peace.

But even as she was the beneficiary of his newfound peace, even as he found newer and more amazing ways to show her his love, and even as she reveled in the incredible sweetness they'd found together, she still had that qualm. The price for this had been his music. And as much as that hurt her, she knew it had to be much, much worse for him.

Was that price too high? If he—

He was gone.

She woke up completely, abruptly.

She had gotten used to never waking up alone. Sometimes they were at Aunt Millie's, sometimes here, but they were always together. At first she'd been loath to leave him alone to deal with the demons he was fighting, but after a while the simple joy of being with him was enough reason. And when he'd vanquished those demons, her happiness was complete. Except for that constant worry that the man she had now wasn't whole, that he had excised a large part of himself and might never heal from the loss, no matter how well he hid it.

Maybe it would just take time, she told herself. But how long? A year? Years?

She sighed inwardly. All she could do was support him, love him, as she had been doing since that day he'd confessed the loss to her. Wholeheartedly, trying to make up for the piece of his heart that was gone.

But now he was gone. And finally she looked at the clock beside the bed. 3:07.

She glanced toward the bathroom door, but she already knew it was open, the room dark. She got up, stifling a yawn. She walked to the bedroom door; perhaps he'd just had trouble sleeping and had gotten up to avoid disturbing her. Given how they'd spent a couple of hours last night, that was hard to believe, but maybe. She glanced into the spare room as she passed the doorway, but it was empty.

Maybe he just got hungry, she thought with a grin. All this activity had to sap a guy's strength.

She pulled the door open. There was no sign of light downstairs in the kitchen, but sometimes you couldn't tell from here. She went down the stairs.

No light. Not in the kitchen or anywhere else.

The possibilities suddenly narrowed down to him sitting in the dark which, although it had happened often before when he was wrestling with the loss of such a huge part of him, hadn't happened lately.

She turned on the under-cabinet lights in the kitchen, which were the softest illumination she could think of.

Nothing.

She looked around for a note, anything that would explain this. Nothing.

A walk, she thought, a tinge of desperation touching her thoughts now. She walked toward the front door, but stopped before she got there, because she could see through the window already that the driveway was empty. The Mustang was no longer where he'd left it last night.

He was gone.

She stood there for a long moment, arguing with herself internally. He'd seemed to be doing so well, but she had to remember what he was going through inwardly. Think of it as if he were having to accept an amputation of a huge part of him, because that's in essence what it was. She'd sensed it came and went, by the times he got quiet and somewhat withdrawn, and trying not to dwell on the irony that he probably only seemed that way by comparison to the rest of the time he was so joyously with her.

She set aside her own pain at that thought; she had to think only of him now. Had to remind herself that while her instinct was to go to him, to comfort him, that might not be what he needed just now.

His way is not your way.

The half-dozen words that echoed in her mind had gotten her through the times when she would have made a wrong move, when she had to consciously chose not to do what she would want done if it was her. If he was out there fighting this alone, because that was his way, she must leave him to do it.

But that didn't mean she couldn't check on him, make sure that's all it was.

She was dressed and pulling her car out of the garage in less than fifteen minutes. She headed for Aunt Millie's, telling herself she would merely go by and make sure the Mustang was there, then make sure he was all right—that being a relative term—and then she would leave him to it. Because she had to. If she'd learned nothing else by almost losing him forever she'd learned that.

He wasn't at Aunt Millie's. The house, repaired now and awaiting fresh paint, sat dark and quiet, the driveway and garage empty.

She turned around, puzzled now. Where on earth would he go at three in the morning? And why would he sneak out without leaving even a note?

Because she didn't know what else to do, she headed back toward her place. Still no Mustang in the drive. She kept going, trying to slow her racing thoughts as she drove. She wasn't really thinking about it when she turned toward town, didn't even realize where she was headed until she saw Booze's statue and realized she was in the town square. Which was, at this hour, as quiet and empty as her house, except for a couple of cars parked here and there.

But not completely dark, she realized, as she saw a faint glow coming from the front window of Booze's Place. That was odd, although she supposed Jake, the manager, could be doing some late—very late—work, stocking or bookkeeping. She turned the car toward the light. Then hit the brakes as she recognized that the muted light seemed to brush gently over an unmistakable, very recognizable shape out front.

The Mustang.

He was here? At Booze's Place? At this hour?

Her mind kicked into high gear, racing through options. She didn't like several of them. An image that reeked of old movies flashed through her mind, of a drunk pounding on the door demanding the bar be opened so he could get a drink. But Jamie didn't drink, not like that. Of course, she didn't have much in the house other than a couple of beers and a bottle or two of wine. Neither she nor True partook much, not after a drunk driver had ripped their lives apart all those years ago.

But that crash had ripped Jamie's life apart, too, so she

couldn't imagine that he'd been hiding a secret addiction only to fall off the wagon here and now.

But it was strange enough that she had to stop, to make sure he was all right. She pulled in beside the Mustang. Got out, walked to the door. She could see the light was coming from the back, the bar area. She tried the front door, which was naturally locked. She walked through the narrow passageway between buildings to the back of the place, sparing a thought for a moment as she always did that she was in Whiskey River, where even at this hour in a dark alley she was relatively safe.

When she reached the back corner and turned, ready to head and see if the back door was open, she instead stopped in her tracks.

She'd almost forgotten about the somewhat battered upright piano that stood along the back wall of the bar section of the place. She never went in there, because it reminded her too strongly of the days Jamie had played there, as a teenager, before Scorpions, when he'd just been that kid everybody looked at warily until he began to play, and then gaped at when he began to sing. He must still have his old door key.

But she was reminded now, powerfully, as music poured out of it. Something she'd never heard before, lilting, airy, yet powerful lower chords building beneath, until the two finally melded into an uplifting climb to a defiantly triumphant crescendo.

Holding her breath, she went to the back door. It was closed, but unlocked. She eased it open. Saw him at the piano, his back to the doorway. Sometimes she forgot he played the piano this well. And that he'd said sometimes it was easier to write music with the fuller range of octaves at his fingertips.

She inched inside, careful to make no noise. She closed the door just in time to hear it begin again, this time with his voice, that wonderful voice, singing lyrics that had already been written on the legal pad beside him. It was a story of love found, lost and regained, but more than that it was about seeing what was really important, and how sometimes you had to nearly lose it all to see it.

She waited until he was done, not only because she wanted to hear it and didn't want to risk interrupting the flow, but also because by the second chorus she was blinking away tears, it was so beautiful.

And then, when he was done and sitting there, taking deep but steady breaths, staring down at his hands on the keys, she finally took those last few steps. And there was no stopping the tears when she read, written across the top of the page in his distinctive half-cursive, half-printed hand, "Zinnia Rose."

Her name hadn't been in the lyrics—Jamie was subtler than that—but the title made it clear. She'd always hated her full name. Until now.

He went very still and she knew he'd sensed her behind

him. She had to swallow hard before she could get any words out. She kept her tone light, so he would know for sure it was a joke.

"I was afraid you were out drinking before dawn."

He didn't look at her. "Catchy. Make a good song."

"Hard to top what I just heard."

He stood then. And when he finally turned to look at her it was all there—the joy, the triumph, everything she'd heard in the music was alive in his eyes.

Her thoughts were tumbling chaotically, and she had no idea where to begin, and so she merely asked, "Why here?"

"My guitar's at Aunt Millie's, and this was closer." He searched her face before saying, rather carefully, "I just woke up with it in my head, and it was so strong I had to try. I didn't want to wake you because I was afraid it would just be…nothing again."

"And instead it's the most beautiful thing you've ever written," she said softly.

"It's good," he agreed tentatively. "Needs some work, but…"

"Is there more?"

The smile that curved his mouth then was like the sun that would be rising soon. "I think so. It feels…damn, it feels good."

He threw his arms around her in a fierce hug. She hugged him back, just as fiercely.

He was whole again.

Chapter Thirty-Three

"STUBBORN THING, THAT muse of yours," Zee said as she handed him a plate of fluffy pancakes and the bottle of syrup. The kind he preferred, had since—and probably because of—his childhood, that had a lot more sugar than maple in it, but since he didn't do it often he didn't worry about it much. But he noted that she had it on hand, even though he knew she preferred the more genuine kind. "Or maybe overworked."

"Maybe," he said as he swallowed the bite he'd just spent a good minute savoring. "More like a contrary kid. She didn't want to play until I said 'Fine, I quit.' Just like Deck told me."

She smiled at him then. "And then she was all, 'Well, if you're going to be that way about it?'"

Jamie grinned. "Pretty much." He took another bite. His appetite had come back along with the music, and with a vengeance. "Although she's liable to get mad at me again when she finds out she's down a notch in the priority list."

Zee stopped in the act of refilling his coffee mug. Set the

pot down. Stared at him.

"What?"

He waved a hand at nothing in particular, that seemed to include everything. "After this. Us."

"You...mean that?"

He put down his fork. He thought she'd known. But then he'd thought that once before, and been very, very wrong.

"If there's anything I've learned out of this, Zee, it's what fed the music. What makes it worth it. This place. And you."

The way she looked at him in that moment made his heart soar as much as the return of the music had. What happened then was well worth the time spent washing sticky maple syrup out of his hair.

And later, when he'd gone back to Aunt Millie's house while Zee ran some errands, he finally felt strong enough. He went to the case that held that precious old acoustic, where he had tucked the letter Zee had given him that day at the storage locker. He pulled it out, stared at it for a moment. Then he looked around the house she had left him, nodded, and looked back. He ran a finger over the writing on the front before he opened the envelope.

Dearest Jamie,

If I know you, and I do, you've put off reading this for a while. And that's all right; a letter from the grave, as it were, requires the right frame of mind. But first things first.

Thank you.

Thank you for making my life so worthwhile, for giving me such joy, filling me with such pride. I never thought to have these things, but you gave them to me a thousand times over. That such happiness could rise out of such pain is no small miracle. And the way you expressed it all in your music was an endless delight to me.

This is not the end I would have chosen, I would much rather have been that little old lady in the front row at one of your shows, with all the youngsters around me wondering what was with the old gal, anyway. But know that I will be there, always, for I believe that music is the connection between this world and whatever other realms there may be, silly and mystical as that sounds. Wherever you are, whatever path your beautiful talent leads you to follow, know that I will be there, ever cheering you on.

You often said you owed me more than you could ever repay. But you're wrong, sweet boy. When I'd nearly given up, you gave me more than I ever hoped to have out of this life.

I do not want this to be a long, weepy screed, so I'll close with two pieces of advice—you knew this was coming, right? One, hang on tight to the one you love, because as you know too well there are no guarantees that the tomorrow in "I'll mend fences tomorrow," will ever come. Two, whenever you're hurting, whenever you're tangled up inside, if you're maybe missing the crazy aunt who loved you so much, you take the Mustang out for a run. It's as close to a hug as I can give you.

I love you, Jamie. And if there's anything that endures forever, it's that.

Aunt Millie

PS: Cut your Zinnia Rose some slack. She'll get there.

He'd never truly laughed and cried at the same time before, but he was doing it now. He wiped at his eyes, and it was hard to breathe because his throat was so tight, but he had to because he was also laughing and needed the air.

He read the letter again.

"I love you, Aunt Millie," he whispered. "Thank you back."

And then he read the PS once more, and this time the laugh won out. Because once again, Aunt Millie had been absolutely right.

"DID THAT GUY find Jamie all right?"

Zee blinked. As usual, she had pretty much tuned out Martha's stream of chatter as she rang up the purchase. She'd been glad to finally have reached the end of her afternoon of errands, anxious to get back to Jamie. So when Martha said his name her inner thoughts and outer reality collided with a jolt.

"What guy?" she asked.

"The one from L.A. The flashy one."

Zee drew back slightly. "Not Boots," she said; although the tall, lanky man had indeed been here from L.A. again last week, nobody on the planet would describe him as flashy.

She'd been glad to see him, to see that the friendship between he and Jamie had survived the breakup of Scorpions. The two men had spent a lot of time together while Boots had been here, and she'd given them plenty of room even though Boots had taken her aside and thanked her.

"With you he's whole again," he'd told her. "You always were the missing piece."

She'd hugged the man for that.

"No," Martha said with a laugh, "not Boots."

Then who? Zee wondered. Leigh, the keyboard player, had been here a couple of days before Boots on her way home to Oklahoma, but since she was obviously female she didn't qualify as the "guy."

"I mean the manager guy who was here an hour or so ago," Martha said.

"Manager?"

Martha frowned. "You know, the band's manager? He said he and Jamie had a lot to talk about, so I figured that was why you were here on your own."

Zee said something, she wasn't even sure what, and escaped the sudden chill of the store into the bright sunshine.

It didn't warm her much.

Her car, gleaming green in the sun, was parked at the end of the row in the small lot. She made it there. Got in. Closed the door. The heat that had built even in the short time she'd been inside surrounded her. Yet she still felt chilled. Made no move, as she normally would, to quickly start the car and turn on the air conditioning.

First Leigh. Then Boots. Now their manager?

And all of this within a week after he'd finally broken through, when new music had begun to flow out of him nearly as fast as ever. Beginning with the song he'd written for her. The song he'd told her was only the latest, because in a way they'd all been written for her.

And with it had come his old energy, the snappingly vivid spark that brought audiences alive, as if he were able to transfer it directly to them in a way few could. He was born for that, and well she knew it. She'd always known it.

And she'd been so overjoyed that the dam had broken that she had forgotten she might be one of the casualties of the flood.

IT TOOK ZEE a while to work up to going out to the house. So long that she began to question what on earth was wrong with her. She ended up chiding herself.

You're afraid of what you'll find.

She had come back to the office and tried to bury herself in work, but since True had only been back to business for a couple of weeks, it only took a couple of hours to get caught up. Even with…distractions, she wasn't behind.

And what distractions they were. Sex on the kitchen table, m'girl?

She found herself grinning. But it faded slightly when she thought of having to live with that kitchen table alone, if he left again. She imagined passing it every day, remembering that morning. She'd had to scrub to get all traces of syrup off of it, but nothing could ever scrub that memory from her mind.

If he left again.

Was there really any *if* about it? He'd gotten what he'd come back here for—his music was back. But…

If there's anything I've learned out of this, Zee, it's what fed the music. What makes it worth it. This place. And you.

That didn't sound like a man who'd be heading back to the bright lights and big city.

She suddenly realized she was pacing. That she'd circled the office at least five times, without doing a thing. That her thoughts were circling in much the same way, chasing each other and never solving anything.

She sat down in the office chair. She had to make herself do it, because what she really wanted to do was go sit on the floor in a corner and wrap her arms around her knees, as if that could protect her. It was what she'd done often in the days after the accident.

True used to find her and coax her out, back to the world she hated just then.

Jamie had quietly joined her.

If there's anything I've learned...

If there was anything she'd learned out of that harrowing time, it was that denial only postponed the inevitable. Hiding in a corner and pretending it hadn't happened had worked for a while, had gotten her to where she could finally face it. Thanks to True's unwavering support. And the fact that Jamie was there, sharing the pain.

That was a bond that would never, ever be broken, no matter what happened now.

And so she gave herself a few minutes, to remember. To think about what had happened in the time Jamie had been home. In a way he'd survived another death, only this time the miracle had happened, that part of him had not died after all, had only gone dormant, exhausted perhaps.

She and Whiskey River had given that back to him.

Perhaps she shouldn't have let herself fall in love with him again. But she laughed at herself even as she thought it; as if she had any choice in the matter. She knew that now. For however long she lived, she would ever and always love Jamie Templeton.

A sound out front drew her gaze. True's truck pulling in next door. And behind him the little blue coupe they'd bought for Hope. They got out and she heard their laughter as, arm in arm, they walked toward his half of the house.

You were determined to take care of him the way he came home and took care of you…

She had been. Especially after Amanda had died. But her brother didn't need her like that anymore.

She felt an odd sort of pressure building inside her as that realization settled in. Life had spun, changed in a huge way, yet again. It always did.

It always did.

But this time, for True, it was good. It was the best.

And for her?

She didn't know. But it was time she found out.

And it was time to trust the man she loved.

Chapter Thirty-Four

IT WAS FINALLY done.

Jamie walked through the house, feeling a sort of satisfaction he hadn't felt in a while, that of a hard, physical job well done. Months of either back-breaking or drudgery, and it was done. Aunt Millie's house—his house—was repaired, clean, furnished, and now, finally, newly painted inside and out, and he'd done most of it himself. The garden still needed some work to return it to its former beauty, but he was going to need help with that. Plants had never been his strong point. It would happen, and in the meantime the house looked like a home again.

Now he just had to make it one.

Even as he thought it he heard a car on the drive. A quick look and a flash of green told him the main element necessary to do that had just arrived.

He practically ran out to greet her. She was looking around, as if searching for something.

"You're just in time. It's official."

There was an oddly tense, silent moment before she said,

"It is?"

"Yep." He waved a hand at the house. "Finished the last of the painting and cleanup this morning. Come on."

"The house. You meant the house."

He looked at her quizzically. "Well, yeah. What else?"

"I thought…you had company."

"Rob?" His brow furrowed. "How'd you hear—" He broke off, laughed. "Never mind. I forgot you went into town. Martha?"

She nodded.

"He mentioned he'd stopped in for directions. And got an earful, I'm sure. But he left an hour ago." Jamie grinned. "I think he was afraid I was going to make him move furniture."

"That was quick."

"Didn't take long," he said. And Rob hadn't been happy.

Zee smiled, but not enough. "You didn't mention he was coming."

He drew back slightly, puzzled by the tightness in her voice. "I didn't know. He just showed up."

"You didn't call him?"

He frowned, still puzzled. "No. Why?"

She shrugged. "After Boots showed up again, and then Leigh, I thought maybe you'd asked him to come. Because…the music is back."

It hit him then. He stared at her, not sure how he felt. "You thought I was…going back? You still don't trust me?"

"I trust you. You aren't—and never were—the problem." She seemed to draw herself up straighter. "I've been doing a lot of thinking."

"Sometimes you do too much. You need to know—"

She held up a hand to stop him. "It's all right," she repeated. "I finally realized that it was my fault. I was the one who threw us away when you left. Because I was afraid to go with you when you asked."

He wasn't sure where she was going with this, but he had no doubt that this was…momentous somehow. He fought down the tension that was building in his gut. Managed to keep his voice even as he said, "Turned out for the best. True needed you, when Amanda got sick."

"Yes. And that tragedy should have taught me how little control I had. But I was still afraid that if I wasn't here, I'd lose what little I had left of my old life." She gave a half-hearted laugh. "I never realized before how ingrained in me it is, to hold on, to try and keep everything the same."

"I get that," he said, softly now. He'd never looked at her need to stay in quite that way, but the moment she said it, he understood. "You were right about one thing. Rob was here to ask me to come back to L.A., put the band back together."

She waited, silently. Asking without asking. And anger kicked in him for a moment. She should know.

And you should have known how she felt when you left.

And then Aunt Millie's words rang in his mind. *Cut your Zinnia Rose some slack. She'll get there.*

He steadied his voice. "Boots, on the other hand, was here to tell me he'd gotten another gig. And Leigh? She came to tell me she was pregnant and they were heading home."

"Oh."

She sounded odd, and for some reason he was remembering all the times he'd found her hiding in a corner, her back to the walls, much as he had been in the emergency room that night.

It was stupid of me to think everyone grieved in the same way. And arrogant to think that way was my way.

She had ever had the grace to apologize when she was wrong, and better, unlike some people, she truly did learn from it.

"You want to know why Rob's visit was so short? Because it doesn't take long to say no."

"But the music—"

He cut her off this time. "I'm not going back to L.A., Zee. It was a grand ride, but it turned out I didn't like the guy I was there very much."

"You're not...still quitting? Music, I mean? You can't," she said, sounding urgent. "You're yourself again. It's who you are, and the world needs it."

"That might be just a little bit grandiose," he said wryly.

"No. It's not."

She said it so firmly he nearly smiled. And the last bit of the anger that had spiked faded. "I'm not quitting. I'm just changing home base. To where it should have been all along." He gave her a lopsided grin. "Rumor has it Texas has a pretty damned fine music scene."

"Of course it does. But touring is—"

"Essential these days. I know. But I made an interesting discovery. It's a heck of a lot easier to get to the rest of the country from Texas than from one of the coasts. And…" His voice trailed off; even now he was almost afraid to ask. Which made him look at the fear that had driven her out here a little differently.

"And?"

"I was hoping this time you might come along. As long as you knew we'd always come home."

She let out a shaky breath. "I was afraid this time you wouldn't ask."

He swallowed. "Is that a yes?"

"It's a hell, yes," she whispered.

He pulled her into his arms. He couldn't regret the tangled path they'd trod to get to here, because he didn't know if they would have gotten here any other way. He just wanted the road to be bright and clear from here on.

After a while he gave her Aunt Millie's letter to read. And watched as she had the same reaction he'd had, crying and laughing at the same time. "And she was right. I did get there."

"Yes. She was. You did," he said, and kissed her.

Much later, in the bed they had decided had to be used despite the smell of fresh paint, he held her close as he said,

"I got some very wise advice once, although I was too young and stupid to take it at the time. From an old hand who came off the road and has his own venue now. He told me if there was someone who made me want to fly right, I should grab her and hang on. You're that for me. You always have been."

"And if I hadn't loved you so much, it would never have hurt for so long. And I wouldn't have been so angry." She nestled against him. "Sometimes I think I had to grow up so fast in some ways that I missed a couple of others."

He rolled onto his side, grinned at her as he cupped a breast. "I dunno. I think you grew up pretty darned perfect."

"I don't need to be perfect," she said, sliding her hand down his body. "Just yours."

He muttered a heartfelt oath as her fingers curled around him. "Always."

The darkness just before dawn found them on the limestone ledge over the river, waiting for the sunrise.

"I'm going to need somebody to handle bookings," he said. "I got a call from one of the guys who runs the music end of South by Southwest in Austin," he said, referring to the one-time local music festival that had grown into something huge and widely known. "And I talked to somebody from Gruene Hall. And a couple of other places."

"So, you just want me for my organizational skills," she teased.

"There is something to be said for your...thorough and

detailed approach," he said, nuzzling the nape of her neck. She had demonstrated that last night; he didn't think there was an inch of his body she'd missed, and the attention she'd paid to some particular inches were etched into his memory forever.

"So I'm a bit of an organization freak."

"A bit?" he said with exaggerated shock. She punched him lightly. He laughed. "I can live with that, as long as it doesn't spill over into my music room."

"Music room?"

"The one I'm going to add on," he said. "And I can guarantee it won't be organized."

"Out of chaos comes creativity?"

"Something like that."

"I can live with that," she said in turn.

He hesitated for one long breath. "Will you?" She turned to look at him as the first light began to brighten the sky. "I know you and True have that place and—"

She cut him off with a finger to his lips. "My brother needed me close then. He doesn't now."

"I do. I always will."

"And I you." She turned her head to glance at the house, the windows beginning to reflect the light of the rising sun. "I think Aunt Millie would like us being here."

"Yes. Because we're proving she was right. We were meant to be."

The sun flared over the horizon and turned the river to

flowing gold. He felt the warmth of it as if it were flowing straight into his heart.

Jamie Templeton was home at last.

The End

The Whiskey River Series

Book 1: *Whiskey River Rescue*

Book 2: *Whiskey River Runaway*

Book 3: *Whiskey River Rockstar*

Available now at your favorite online retailer!

Love the town of Whiskey River, Texas? Stay awhile. Where the women are feisty, the men are sexy and the romance is hotter than ever.

The Brothers of Whiskey River Series

If you enjoyed **Whiskey River Runaway**, you'll love the other Whiskey River stories!

Book 1: **Texas Heirs** by Eve Gaddy and Katherine Garbera

Book 2: **Texas Cowboy** by Eve Gaddy

Book 3: **Texas Tycoon** by Katherine Garbera

Book 4: **Texas Rebel** by Eve Gaddy

Book 5: **Texas Lover** by Katherine Garbera

Book 6: **Texas Bachelor** by Eve Gaddy and Katherine Garbera

Available now at your favorite online retailer!

About the Author

Author of more than 70 books, (she sold her first ten in less than two years) Justine Davis is a five time winner of the coveted RWA RITA Award, including for being inducted into the RWA Hall of Fame. A fifteen time nominee for RT Book Review awards, she has won four times, received three of their lifetime achievement awards, and had four titles on the magazine's 200 Best of all Time list. Her books have appeared on national best seller lists, including USA Today. She has been featured on CNN, taught at several national and international conferences, and at the UCLA writer's program.

After years of working in law enforcement, and more years doing both, Justine now writes full time. She lives near beautiful Puget Sound in Washington State, peacefully coexisting with deer, bears, a pair of bald eagles, a tailless raccoon, and her beloved '67 Corvette roadster. When she's not writing, taking photographs, or driving said roadster (and yes, it goes very fast) she tends to her knitting. Literally.

Visit Justine at her website at JustineDavis.com.

Thank you for reading

Whiskey River Rockstar

If you enjoyed this book, you can find more from all our great authors at TulePublishing.com, or from your favorite online retailer.

Made in the USA
Lexington, KY
07 July 2018